To David

The Mystery of the

I hope you take a break from soccer to give this book a read. Have a great time!

The Mystery of the

Graffiti Ghoul

Marty Chan

thistledown press

Library and Archives Canada Cataloguing in Publication

Chan, Marty
The mystery of the graffiti ghoul / Marty Chan.

ISBN-10 1-897235-00-3
ISBN-13 978-1-897235-00-3

1. Chinese Canadians–Juvenile fiction. I. Title.

PS8555.H39244M983 2006   jC813'.54   C2006-900057-3

Cover illustration by Laura Lee Osborne
Cover and book design by Jackie Forrie
Typeset by Thistledown Press

Thistledown Press Ltd.
633 Main Street
Saskatoon, Saskatchewan, S7H 0J8
www.thistledownpress.com

Canada Council   Conseil des Arts
for the Arts   du Canada

SASKATCHEWAN
ARTS BOARD

Canadian   Patrimoine
Heritage   canadien

Thistledown Press gratefully acknowledges the financial assistance of the Canada Council for the Arts, the Saskatchewan Arts Board, and the Book Publishing Industry Development Program of the Department of Canadian Heritage for its publishing program.

ACKNOWLEDGEMENTS

For their insights I owe my left arm to Diane Tucker, Michelle Chan, Brad Smilanich, Wei Wong, and Joe Tucker. For their random acts of kindness, I owe my right arm to Robb Wynn, Peter Edwards, Laura Lee Osborne, Norm & Janet Sasseville, Jim Turner, Margo Johnston, Laurier and Terry Jule, Danny Chan, Corinne St. Denis, the Nancies, Laurie Goss, Leann Laroque, Lena Bourgeois, Brenda London, Ann Blakely, Pat Lore, Maureen Thomas, Marilyn Stevenson, Launa Matichuk, Margaret Roshko, Margaret Doran, and CBC Radio. I'd like also like to thank my test audiences: the students and staff at Dovercourt, G.H. Primeau, G.P. Vanier, Lymburn, Meyonohk, Notre Dame, S. Bruce Smith, Hazeldean, and Waverly. Finally, to the fashion designer who created corduroy pants: thanks for the nightmares!

The Mystery of the

ONE

I'd rather have gone naked than shop for clothes with my mom, because she had a talent for finding shirts older than fossils. Like a palaeontologist digging up dinosaur bones, she discovered ancient pants in bargain caves. If I wore the outdated sweaters she picked, I'd become extinct faster than a woolly mammoth.

Being the only Chinese kid at school already made me stand out like a beach ball on a snow bank. My black hair and darker skin made me different from the rest of the kids, and my classmates teased me almost every day. They called me a math geek. They claimed I ate cats. They said Jackie Chan was my uncle. None of it was true, but that didn't stop them from making up nasty rumours about me. When I showed up at school in the clothes my mom bought, the teasing got worse. Much worse.

Since everyone at school wore blue jeans, I figured if I could get a pair of those I'd be able to blend in with the crowd. With nice clothes, I could fit in. I could become the cool guy, the popular boy, the kid no one teased. On the far wall of the boys' clothing section at Sears, a pair of jeans that would make me normal waited to be picked up, but Mom dragged me away before I could even touch the denim of my dreams.

"Cost too much," she said.

"Mom, I'm ten years old," I said. "Don't you think I'm old enough to pick my own pants?"

"I pay, I pick."

"But I'm the one who has to wear them," I argued. "I don't want to look stupid."

"You not have to worry. I not make you look dumb. Now hold my purse."

Mom tossed me her shiny red bag, but I let it drop to the floor. Her idea of dumb and mine were as different as chocolate bars and tofu patties. She dipped her bony hands into an aquamarine pond of bargain clothes and reeled in a purple T-shirt that had teddy bears dancing across the chest.

"Aiya. Too small," she muttered. She shook her head, her mass of curly black hair swinging back and forth on her head like a football helmet that was too big.

She tossed the shirt back and grabbed a pair of pink and blue overalls with sunflowers stitched into the bib.

"What about this one?" Mom asked.

"I think they're for girls," I said.

"Boy, girl. If it fit, what does it matter?"

It mattered. It *really* mattered. How could she not see the difference between girl and boy clothes? Either she was an alien from another planet where everyone looked exactly alike, or Mom's job was to make my life miserable. Since I never found enough proof of her alien origins, I had to guess that Mom's salary went up every time she humiliated me. She was going to get rich on this shopping trip.

"Aiya, they're ripped," she said.

Back the overalls went. Mom dug through the rest of the pile, the ugliest clothes ever made by humans or aliens. Nothing caught her eye. Maybe all the clothes were ripped. Maybe they were too small. Maybe my luck would hold out and I'd escape the fashion freaks on the bargain table.

"Ah," she said. "These are the pants for you." She fished out a pair of plaid slacks and checked the length against my legs.

I got dizzy just looking at the criss-crossing lines and multicoloured patches. They looked like a tic-tac-toe board that had spun out of control.

"I think I'm allergic to them," I said.

She ignored me. "They look nice."

"Mom, I think I saw some blue jeans on sale," I said.

"The cheapest clothes are here," she declared.

Only rejects ended up on the bargain table. They were like the last kid picked to play basketball. The team captains snapped up the good players first, but at the end there was always one kid left standing — the klutz who couldn't dribble, the doofus who scored on his own net, the loser who had to be picked because the captain had no other choice. That left-over kid was usually me. Now *I* was the captain, and I had no choice but to pick the leftover plaid pants.

"What you waiting for?" Mom held up the pants. Her jade bracelet slipped up her wrist and disappeared under her sleeve. I wished I could disappear just as easily. "They look cute."

"Mom, I don't want to look cute. I want to look grown up."

"They make you look grown up too."

"They do not."

She pointed to a grey-haired man slouched over a table, picking up a wool sweater with his wrinkled hands. He wore an identical pair of plaid pants.

I didn't want to look that old, I thought. Why didn't Mom shop for cool pants? Why did she always have to look for bargains? Why did we have such different tastes in everything?

Mom sighed. "Okay, okay. I picked one pair. You can pick a pair."

"Alright!" I yelled. A helicopter of hope took off for the clear blue denim skies. "Now you're talk — "

"From *this* table," Mom interrupted.

My helicopter crashed into the bright sea of corduroy and polyester.

"Mom, can I at least try on a pair of jeans?"

"Only bad boys wear blue jeans."

"Like who?" I asked.

"Never mind. You not get jeans."

"Why?"

"Because."

"Because why?" A few more "whys" and she might let me try on blue jeans.

"Because I say so," she growled.

"Because you say so *why*?"

Mom's eyebrows arched up like bat wings. "Why do you keep saying that?" she asked.

"Because," I answered.

"Because *why*?" she asked. Mom had turned my own trick against me.

I said nothing, crossing my arms over my chest.

"Try them on," Mom insisted, holding out the pants. She might as well have been offering a spoonful of bitter cough medicine.

"I'm not wearing them," I said.

"You will."

"I don't want to."

"Put them on. Now."

"You can't make me," I said. "I hate plaid pants."

Standoff. Mom wouldn't back down and neither would I. But then she resorted to a negotiation tactic that all mothers use to win arguments: "Marty, how you know you hate plaid pants if you never try them on?"

A few weeks ago she'd used the same question when I refused to eat gai lan, a Chinese broccoli that smelled like the bottom of my feet. When I couldn't answer her then, I had to eat the bitter vegetable. Today, I had to think of an answer to Mom's tricky question or else I'd have to try on the pants.

"Because . . . " I said, stalling for time.

But before I could say another word Mom slunk over beside me, grabbed my pants by the belt loops and yanked them down to my ankles.

"Mom!" I yelped.

"Now will you try on the new pants?" she asked.

I couldn't argue with her, standing in the middle of the busy department store in my tighty whities. I covered myself with the plaid pants.

"Try these too." She tossed me a pair of green corduroys.

I slapped the cords against my butt and shuffled across the carpet, my own pants still hanging around my ankles like leg irons. When I touched the metal door knob, electricity bit my hand.

"Ouch." I pulled away. Shuffling across the carpet had built up a static charge in my body. How was I going to open the door without getting another shock?

"Do you need help?" Mom asked.

"No, I'm okay." Using the pants as antistatic mittens, I opened the door.

The dressing room was tinier than a bathroom stall. Hanging on a beige wall, a tall narrow mirror reflected my skinny, half-naked body. I inched past the minefield of metal pins on the floor and kicked off my shoes and pants.

Outside the door, Mom ordered, "Try the plaid pants on first."

Instead I slipped on the corduroys, zipped up the fly and fastened the button. Take that, Mom, I thought. But then I caught a glimpse of myself in the mirror — the corduroys were even grosser than the plaid pants. They were the ugliest pants in the universe! First of all, they were five sizes too big. Second, they were super-bright neon green. And worst of all, incredibly thick fuzzy rows sprouted all the way down the legs. It looked like my pants needed to be mowed.

Forget it. I wouldn't wear the lawn for another minute. I started to undo the top button, but before I could unzip, Mom kicked open the dressing room door, grabbed my arm and dragged me into the middle of the busy store.

"These aren't the plaid pants," she said.

"I know, Mom. I'll change right now."

"No. Wait. These are perfect." She beamed. "We should buy them."

If the kids from school spotted me in these fuzzy pants, they'd get their fully-charged cattle prods to herd me into the geek corral where I'd end up on display for all to taunt and tease. I scanned the store for familiar faces. Around me, moms and sons shopped for cool clothes. Across the aisle, the grey-haired man in the plaid pants examined a pair of black dress socks. So far so good. I saw no one I knew.

Then I noticed someone in the girls' clothing section. At first I didn't want to look, but like picking a scab, the itch to peek got the better of me, and once I did I wished I'd left well enough alone. There was Trina Brewster — the biggest gossip in grade four and my worst enemy. As Trina sifted through blouses and sipped a slushie through a bendy straw, I wondered how someone so pretty could act so mean. She constantly teased me for being Chinese. She picked on me for wiping my nose on my sleeve. She made fun of my thick glasses. Sometimes she didn't even need a reason; she just teased me because she felt like it. Why did Trina have to be at Sears, today of all days? I had to hide.

Before I could move, Mom let out an air-raid-siren screech. "Pull your pants up! I can see your underwear."

Every head in the store turned toward us. The boys snickered. The moms smiled. The grey-haired man hiked up his plaid pants. I jumped behind a rack of shirts. From between the hangers I watched Trina as she scanned the store. *Don't look this way*, I thought, sending telepathic signals for her to go back to drinking her slushie. It worked. She resumed checking the blouses on the rack.

Something started to tug on my pant legs. The pants slipped down a couple of inches. I clutched the top of the pants, stopping them from dropping any further. What was going on? There was Mom kneeling on the carpet, rolling up the pant legs.

"What are you doing?" I whispered.

"They a little long, but you grow into them," she said, far too loudly.

"Mom," I said. "Quit it."

I hitched the pants up.

"Maybe you need a belt," she suggested.

"Shhhh," I hissed.

"Why you want me to be quiet?"

"I'll explain later."

"Tell me now!"

"Please, Mom," I begged.

Too late. Trina walked in front of me and smiled like a cat that'd caught a mouse. "Oh, hi, Marty. I thought I heard you. I see you're shopping with your *mommy.*"

Mom stood up. "Marty, who is this?"

I just glared at Trina and said nothing.

"I'm Trina Brewster. Marty and I are in the same class."

"Nice to meet you," Mom said.

Trina noticed my legs. "Marty, are these your new pants?"

I was sure that a cruel comment teetered on the tip of Trina's orange-stained tongue. As long as I didn't admit the pants were mine, she couldn't make fun of me. I said nothing.

Mom nudged me. "Talk to your friend."

"She's not my friend," I growled.

Mom sighed. "Marty say he not like these pants. I don't think we will get them."

She didn't think we'd get them? At last something went my way.

Trina's freckled face lit up. "Don't put them back, Mrs. Chan. I think you've picked out a great pair of pants."

Mom looked at me. "See, Marty? You have nothing to worry about. Your friend likes them."

Trina smiled wickedly. She didn't like the pants; she just wanted my mom to buy them so that all the kids could make fun of me.

"Mrs. Chan, I'm sure Marty will be the talk of the town in these pants."

"Thank you, Trina," Mom said.

"See you at school on Monday, Marty. I hope you'll wear your new pants." Trina sucked her swamp water slushie through her bendy straw. "Mmm, that's good," she said, grinning evilly as she turned and sauntered away.

Her blonde ponytail swished back and forth like the pendulum on the Grandfather Clock of Doom, ticking off my last seconds of being normal. I wished Trina'd take another sip of the slushie and get a brain freeze so powerful that it wiped out her memory. But good things like that only happened to people in blue jeans. Not to me.

TWO

As soon as Mom and I came home from shopping, I stuffed the neon green corduroy pants in my sock drawer. I could never find socks that matched, and I was sure it was because a sock monster lived in my drawer and ate one sock a week. I hoped the monster would swallow my new pants. Just to be sure, I moved all my socks into the closet so the sock monster would have nothing but the corduroys to feed on.

But on Monday morning the pants had crawled out of the drawer, slithered on top of my bed, crawled across my Spider-Man blanket and climbed up my legs. I kicked them to the floor before they could completely wrap around me. I peeked over the edge of the mattress. On the floor, the pants seemed to curl around the leg of the bed like a fuzzy python. The pants had survived the sock monster and now they were after me.

Mom knocked on my bedroom door and shouted, "Marty, you wear the new pants today."

"I can't find them," I lied.

"I took them out of your drawer. They on your bed. You see them?"

So Mom had rescued the pants from the sock monster. I scrambled out of bed and scooped them up. "No, I don't see them anywhere."

"You want me to help you look?"

"No!" I shouted.

The pants had to disappear fast, or else I'd be stuck wearing them to school. Maybe I could stick them under my mattress.

Mom yelled, "Don't make your bed. I wash the sheets today."

Was she reading my mind? I had to hide the pants somewhere other than my bedroom. Our family lived in the back of a grocery store, which gave my parents a chance to save money by working and living in the same place, and which also gave me a chance to hide the pants in one of the store's many nooks and crannies. But first I had to sneak past Mom.

Stalling for time, I yelled, "Mom, can you make blueberry pancakes for breakfast?"

"I already make *jook*," she said. "Hurry up before it get cold."

Jook was hot rice porridge, the blandest breakfast food in the world. Even though our store had pancake mix, syrup and blueberries, Mom cooked only *jook* for breakfast. She claimed it was good for me; I thought she made me eat it because she worried that pancakes would turn my eyes round, just like she worried that watching too much TV would turn my eyes square.

"I'll be out in a minute," I yelled. "I have to find the pants."

I could hear Mom walk toward the kitchen. My chance! I balled up the corduroys, jammed them under my Hong Kong tourist T-shirt, which doubled as my pyjama top, and cracked open my door. The coast was clear. I stepped into the hallway and crept to the best hiding spot in the grocery store.

On a shelf of unsold oatmeal raisin cookies, I hid the stuff I didn't want my parents to find: UFO magazines, my walkie-talkie; now I could hide the corduroy pants there. Not many people shopped at our store since the IGA had opened a couple of blocks away, but even our long-time customers knew better than to buy the stale cookies that had been around since even before my parents bought the store. The yellow packages were like the Great Wall of China, hiding forbidden treasures behind them.

"Marty, where you going?" Mom asked. Like a silent ninja, she had snuck up behind me.

"Uh, I don't feel well. I have to use the bathroom," I said.

"What's wrong?" Mom spun me around. "Aiya."

She poked at my swollen belly that stretched out the drawing of a Chinese junk on the front of my T-shirt, but I stepped back before she could sink my plan. I clutched my stomach and doubled over.

"I think I ate too much rice last night," I said.

"I can fix that," she said, coming toward me. "I rub your stomach with Tiger Balm."

Tiger Balm stunk like the inside of my belly button and felt like warm *jook* when the thick ointment was slathered on my skin. Mom used the stuff whenever I was sick and threatened to use it whenever she suspected I was pretending to be sick.

"Let's see your belly, Marty."

"Mom, I could explode any minute."

Before I could get away, she lifted my shirt. The pants fell out and plopped on my bare feet. I wanted to crawl under them.

"You feel better now?" Mom asked.

"Oh, *that's* where the pants are. I was looking all over for them."

"Good thing we find them. Hold your leg up. I put them on for you."

"Mom, I can get dressed myself."

"Do it," she barked.

I put a hand on her shoulder to balance myself and lifted my leg. Within a few seconds the pants were on and my fate was sealed.

On my way to school I decided to dull the pants' nerdy shine. I jumped in a puddle just outside the Bouvier Drugstore. Then I rubbed myself against the side of a muddy pickup truck until I noticed the driver was still inside. I ran down the Main Street sidewalk before she could get out of the truck. When I reached the chain-link fence that surrounded the school, I tried to snag the pants on a stray wire, but those corduroys were made to last. Taking the long way around the school fence, I looked for anything to destroy the pants, but found nothing. I was running out of hope.

In my dark hour, I turned to the Church. The red brick building, crowned by the tall silver steeple, sat beside the school, and I remembered our town priest, Father Sasseville, saying that the Church had answers to every problem. The answer to my problem lay in the shadow of the steeple: a flowerless garden bed.

I mashed my knees in the frosty soil until the pants started to stain. Hallelujah! My plan was working. I ground my knees into the dirt harder. Then the church doors swung open. Father Sasseville stepped out onto the cement porch, adjusting his white collar. He spotted me kneeling in his garden.

"My son, if you want to pray, better to do it inside the church."

I stood up. "Yes, sir."

"What are you doing?"

"Looking for a miracle," I mumbled, stepping off the dirt.

"Did you find it?"

"Just about," I said. "See you later, Father Sasseville."

"Wait. Your pants are filthy." He pulled out a large handkerchief. "Don't worry. This will take the dirt out."

"I like my pants this way," I said.

But before I could run off, Father Sasseville stopped me and wiped the grime that I had worked in between the corduroy ribs.

"So why were you really in the garden bed?" he asked.

"I tripped," I lied, remembering he had an out-of-this-world alliance with my parents and that anything I said to him would probably get back to them.

"Watch where you're walking next time, Marty." He folded his handkerchief. "There. Almost as good as new."

The stains looked like freckles — dirty but not quite dirty enough.

"They're nice pants," he continued. "I'm sure you'll turn a few girls' heads," he called after me.

Father Sasseville was right. I'd be turning a lot of girls' heads. They'd be turning and laughing. I shambled toward the school. Outside the fence gate, I scanned the school ground, hoping it would be empty. No such luck.

French and English languages split my school in two, with the French classes on the north side and the English classes on the south side. Even the schoolyard was divided. The French kids played on their end of the schoolyard and the English students stayed on their own turf. An invisible French-English border started at the crack in the wall between the windows of Mrs. Riopel's classroom, stretched across the lawn between two prairie dog holes and ended at the stone statue of Jesus in the middle of the schoolyard. Everyone called this border "The Line."

In the past the French and English kids had gathered on either side of The Line to wage snowball wars or chicken fights every recess and lunch hour, but Principal Henday ended the schoolyard battles with the threat of instant detention. Now The Line represented an uneasy peace between the English and the French. On one side of The Line, the French boys played tag, trying to impress the French girls, while on the other side English boys took turns jumping into a pile of fallen leaves, trying to impress the English girls.

My big break. With no one looking my way, I scooted through the fence gate and hustled toward the school. I willed everyone to look away, trying to become as invisible as The Line.

From across the yard Trina Brewster bellowed, "There he is!"

I picked up the pace, but it was too late. The English girls rushed toward me, followed by the guys. The French kids turned and gawked.

Eric Johnson cut me off. "Gross! It looks like someone puked on your legs!"

The French kids moved closer. Jean and Jacques Boissonault, the twin bullies, closed in on me. They were Father Sasseville's altar boys and guardians of his secrets, but they behaved more like devils than angels, teasing and torturing me every day. No day was complete until they'd shoved me into a locker, dumped worms down my shirt or washed my glasses in toilet water.

Jean laughed. "Chinaboy's got celery legs!"

Jacques slapped his stocky brother. "Good one."

Jean's green eyes lit up. He had more than one insult in him this morning. "It looks like a Chia Pig exploded on his legs."

Giggles rippled through the crowd.

Eric scratched his spiky blond hair and asked, "What's a Chia Pig?"

"It looks like a tiny piggy bank," Jacques explained, "but little plants grow on its skin."

Eric muttered, "I still think his pants look like puke."

Stanley Ross, the class clown with elephant ears, pointed at me. "You've got broccoli butt."

The kids laughed loudly.

Stanley's ears flapped as he chanted at me, "Broccoli butt! Broccoli butt!"

Soon everyone was chanting, "Broccoli butt!"

My face burned bright red, but there was no escape. The kids surrounded me, laughing and pointing. I tried to remember the advice Ms. Hawkins, my grade four teacher, once gave me. If *I* laughed at cruel jokes about me, she said, people wouldn't find the jokes so funny. She said a smile could be a force field against the worst insults. I twisted my lips into a smile.

"Broccoli butt, broccoli butt!" the kids chanted.

"That's funny!" I shouted.

The chanting stopped. The kids looked at one another, unsure of what to do. I started to laugh.

"Broccoli butt," I said. "It's hilarious."

My force field was working. The kids stopped laughing now that they saw the teasing didn't bug me. Of course their teasing did bother me, but I couldn't let them know it. I kept laughing. Trina stepped out from the crowd. Here was the true test; I couldn't let my force field drop.

"Did you know that Marty's *mommy* picked out his special pants?" she said.

Her laser beam insult sliced through my shield. My smile weakened.

"She dresses him too. Doesn't she, Marty?"

If Trina had said this any other day but today, it wouldn't have been true. My force field dropped lower.

She chanted, "Mommy's boy! Mommy's boy!"

The other kids repeated the chant until my force field shattered into a million pieces around my broken smile. My eyes started to well up with tears, which would wash away the last bit of my protection against the kids' taunts.

"Hey," a boy called out. "How does Trina know Marty went shopping with his mom?"

Remi Boudreau stepped out of the crowd. He was a star hockey player, the coolest French kid at school and my only friend in the galaxy.

"I saw them in the store," she replied.

"Oh?" Remi folded his arms over his Montreal Canadiens hockey jersey. "What were *you* doing there?"

"Shopping," Trina said.

Samantha McNally backed her friend. "Why don't you keep your big nose out of Trina's business, French Fry?" she said.

Actually, Remi was built more like a baked potato; Samantha was the one who looked like a french fry — a french fry covered in ketchup lipstick with mustard pigtails.

Remi ignored Samantha's insult, his force field stronger than mine. "Marty, did you see Trina shopping at the store?"

What was he up to? I said nothing.

"Was she following you?" He cracked his neck to the left, then back to the right and yawned, covering his mouth with both hands — his signal to play along.

"I think she might have been," I said.

The other kids gasped. Trina squirmed as she looked around at the crowd.

Remi paced around Trina. "So, does she follow you everywhere?"

"Yes," I declared, starting to grin.

"I do not," Trina protested.

"Then why were you at the store?" asked Eric.

Samantha piped up. "It's called window shopping, Eric."

"Why does she want to buy windows?" Eric wondered.

Remi shook his head. "Duh. It's a lie. She wants Marty to be her boyfriend."

"What?" Trina coughed. "Him? No way! I'd rather go out with someone from the trailer park."

The kids gasped. Lawrence Bennet, the king of trivia, said, "But only criminals live there."

"And single moms," Samantha added. "And I heard that the people in — "

"Forget those lies," Remi snapped. "Marty turned down Trina, and that's why she's being a monkey butt."

"No one turns me down," Trina said.

Samantha screwed up her face. "Ew, you want Marty to be your boyfriend."

"No," Trina said. "The French kid's making stuff up."

Eric shook his head. "I don't get it. Who wants to buy windows?"

Samantha swacked Eric on the arm. "There are no windows. Trina was following Marty."

Trina shouted, "It was a coincidence that we were at the store at the same time!"

Remi shook his head. "Is coincidence another word for following?"

Trina's face turned purple. "I was not following him!"

Jean Boissonault laughed. "*Anglais* girls are crazy."

Anglais was what the French kids called the English kids, and no one ever used the word in a nice way.

"I'm not crazy," Trina protested. "I don't even like him. He smells like garlic and he picks his nose when he thinks people aren't looking."

No one listened to her. They were too busy chattering among themselves. The kids broke off into small groups, gossiping about Trina's crush. She chased after her friends, trying to tell her side of the story, but no one was interested; rumours sounded way better.

Remi flapped his arms three times — a signal for me to go with him — then jogged toward the far end of the school. Because Remi was French and I went to school with the English, we had to pretend that we weren't friends. Last year some kids spotted us hanging out together and decided that anyone who was caught "Crossing The Line" would be punished. The Boissonault brothers tortured the French traitors, while Eric Johnson dealt with English turncoats. Line Crossers received ninety-nine nurples, but no guy could stand more than twenty-three nipple twists before he begged for mercy. After Remi and I paid the painful price for Crossing The Line, we decided to hide our friendship at school. When I was sure no one was looking my way, I joined my pal.

"I owe you one," I said.

"The monkey butt had it coming."

"She's going to get you back for what you said," I warned.

"She doesn't scare me."

"Well, she scares me," I said.

"All Trina does is make up stories about people. They're just words. You know that saying? Sticks and stones may break my bones, but words'll never hurt me."

I couldn't agree. "You can say that because no one ever says bad things about *you*."

"Forget Trina. We have bigger things to worry about," Remi said. "Check this out."

He led me between a leafless hedge and a row of pine trees to the school's equipment shed. I usually avoided the wooden shed because it smelled funky — I thought an old cat had climbed into the building and died. I couldn't tell for sure, though, because the shed doors were usually padlocked. But today the padlock was lying on the dirt pathway beside a broken beer bottle and a can of spray paint. The doors were wide open.

"Was anything stolen?"

"I don't think so. There's nothing in there that's worth taking."

Blue high jump mats took up most of the space in the shed. Beside them, the high jump bars leaned against a wall along with a couple of rakes, a bag of deflated soccer balls and some orange pylons.

"Why did they do this?" I asked.

"That's not the half of it," Remi said.

He swung the wooden doors shut. A little part of the left door had been broken off, probably from someone ripping off the lock. Across both doors, someone had spray-painted multicoloured squiggly lines, spirals and half-finished star designs. In the centre of the graffiti was a message:

GHOUL RULE

The letters were red, outlined with black. "Ghoul" was painted across the left door and "Rule" was on the other one. The words bulged like cartoon tires filled with too much air.

"Who did this?" I asked.

"That's what I'd like to know," a stern voice said behind us. We turned slowly around. There stood Principal Henday and he did not look happy.

THREE

"**D**oes one of you want to explain this?" Mr. Henday asked.

"It wasn't us," Remi said.

"We found it like this," I added.

Our principal ran his hand over his bald head and sighed deeply. "I thought you boys knew better."

"It's the truth. We didn't do it," I exclaimed. "You have to believe me, Principal Henday."

To his face we called him by his real name, but behind his back all the kids called Mr. Henday "The Rake," because he was tall and skinny and had big feet, which made him look like a human rake. I wondered if he'd find his nickname funny; I didn't want to be the one to ask. The Rake folded his arms and tapped his index finger against his elbow.

If Principal Henday wanted someone to confess, all he had to do was keep quiet and tap that finger of interrogation. One time David Field accidentally kicked a soccer ball through a school window. The Rake lined up all the boys in the gym and told us that someone was going to confess to the crime. Then he stood back and tapped his finger against his elbow. By tap two hundred and eighteen, David broke down and confessed to breaking the window, cheating off my math test and wetting his bed. The Rake's finger had awesome power against the guilty. So even though Remi and I were innocent, my stomach fluttered and my knees shook. I felt the sudden urge to confess to a crime that I didn't commit. Remi broke into a sweat. The Rake noticed and tapped faster.

"Mr. Boudreau, how many strikes do you have against you?" Mr. Henday asked.

"One," mumbled Remi.

The Rake handed out strikes to kids who misbehaved. One strike meant one day's detention. Two strikes meant a week's worth of detention. Three strikes and The Rake called the student's parents. The strike Remi already had wasn't even his fault. Eric Johnson had dumped a glass of water down my back and Remi had come to my rescue. He soaked Eric with a jug of water just as Mrs. Riopel walked into the lunchroom. When she saw the empty water jug in Remi's hands and the water dripping off Eric's blond hair, she freaked out. I told her Remi was standing up for me, but she still gave him a strike. Eric received a strike as well, which brought his total to two. Eric stopped dumping water on me after that.

"The graffiti will be strike two, Mr. Boudreau."

"I didn't do it," Remi said.

"Once a troublemaker, always a troublemaker," Mr. Henday said.

It wasn't fair for him to assume that Remi was a troublemaker because of one strike. That was like kids assuming that I knew kung fu because I looked Chinese.

"I can only wait so long, Mr. Boudreau."

Like a nearsighted umpire, The Rake was about to make a bad call. I had to stop him.

"Mr. Henday, you're wrong about Remi," I said.

"How would you know, Mr. Chan? Did you have a hand in the crime?"

If I did do it, my hands would be covered with paint, but the graffiti was dry, and my hands were clean. "Remi couldn't have painted the graffiti," I said. "If he did, the paint would still be wet."

The Rake walked to the graffitied doors. He dragged his finger across the message. It came away dry.

"Mr. Boudreau could have painted this over the weekend."

"I was visiting my grandma in St. Paul this weekend," Remi said. "You can check with my parents if you don't believe me."

"You were there the whole weekend?" Principal Henday folded his arms and tapped his elbow.

Remi nodded. "We got back late last night."

"Mr. Boudreau, would you like me to check that story with your parents?"

"They'll tell you the same thing."

The Rake tapped his finger another seventeen times, but Remi stared at him, not blinking or sweating. Finally, The Rake gave up.

"Okay, I believe you, but from now on, you should report this kind of thing to a teacher or to me right away."

He glared at both of us.

"Yes, Mr. Henday," we said.

"You'd better get to class. The bell is going to ring in . . . " He checked his watch. "Three . . . two . . . one."

The bell rang. At our school, everything ran on The Rake's time. We walked away from the shed.

Out of Mr. Henday's earshot, Remi leaned over and whispered, "That was pretty smart to notice the paint was dry."

"You were the one who found the graffiti in the first place," I said.

"I guess we make a good team."

"You bet, Remi. I'm the brains. You're the brawn."

"Yeah . . . what's brawn?"

"It's why I'm the brains," I said. "It means you're the muscle."

Remi flexed his arm and kissed his bicep.

"Don't let it go to your head," I said.

"So who do you think painted the graffiti?" Remi asked.

"Someone named Ghoul."

"Duh! I knew that. I meant who is this guy?"

I shrugged. "Someone who doesn't write very well. He should have written an 'S' at the end of 'Rule'."

"Maybe he ran out of paint," Remi suggested.

I nodded. "Ghoul's a pretty weird name. Who would name their kid that?"

"It's a nickname," Remi suggested. "But who looks like a ghoul?"

I shrugged. "Maybe he acts like a ghoul."

"Or he sounds like a ghoul," Remi guessed.

"What does a ghoul sound like?"

Remi thought for a second. "My dad has a CD by Leonard Cohen. That guy definitely sounds like a ghoul."

"What's he sound like?"

Remi growled very slowly and with no emotion in his voice: "He so-o-ounds like a ro-o-obot with a baa-a-d co-o-o-old."

"Creepy," I said. "Does anyone at school sound like that?"

Remi cleared his throat and talked normally. "We'll have to check."

"Okay," I said.

"Do you think The Rake will wipe out the strike against me if we find Ghoul?"

"You didn't deserve the strike in the first place."

"It'd be great to wipe it out," Remi said. "All we have to do is catch this Ghoul guy."

"He's not just a Ghoul. He's a Graffiti Ghoul."

He nodded. "That should be our code name for him."

"Sure," I said.

"There's no way Graffiti Ghoul can hide from us for long. You're the brains. I'm the prawn."

I laughed. "I think you want to be the brawn, not the prawn."

"Why?"

"A prawn is a shrimp," I replied.

"Good to know." Remi blushed. "I'll check out the French kids. We'll report back at recess."

"Keep a low profile," I said. "We don't want to bring too much attention to ourselves."

When I walked into my homeroom all the kids started to sing: "Marty and Trina sitting in a tree, K.I.S.S.I.N.G. First comes love, then comes marriage. Then comes Marty with a baby carriage!"

My face turned orange like a cooked crab shell and I scuttled into my seat. A tidal wave of laughter washed around me, but I clung to the sides of my desk, bracing against the storm. What could be worse than being married to my worst enemy? I thought about living in the same house with her insulting me morning, noon and night. I imagined her chewing strawberry bubble gum and sticking the used pieces on my pillow. Did the gum make her lips taste like strawberries? The only way to know for sure was to kiss her. Ew. To drown out the image of us kissing, I tried to think other thoughts: a cat coughing up a hairball, my mom cleaning up the hairball, a garbage can full of hairballs with pieces of gum stuck in them . . . the gum was strawberry, the same strawberry bubble gum that Trina chewed just before she kissed me. Double ew!

The real Trina walked into the classroom. She wasn't chewing strawberry gum and it didn't look like she wanted to kiss me.

Eric Johnson started to sing, "Trina and Marty sitting in a tree, K.I.S.Sssssssss . . . "

Trina shot a glare at him, sucking air through her flared nostrils like a vacuum cleaner set on high. Eric ducked down in his desk and shut up. She scanned the classroom, waiting for someone else to sing. No one did.

Ms. Hawkins stepped into the room behind Trina. "Take your seat. Class is about to start."

"The other kids are making fun of me," Trina said.

"Which kids?" Ms. Hawkins asked.

"Everyone," Trina whined. "They're being really mean. I think you should make them all buy me a slushie to apologise."

"Sit down, Trina. I'll deal with this."

Trina headed to her desk while Ms. Hawkins tied her long blonde hair into a ponytail and plucked a pencil from her desk top.

Ms. Hawkins slowly twirled her pencil in the air. "I'm very disappointed."

Our teacher never got mad. She just got "disappointed," which made me feel worse than if she yelled.

"I think you all need to write an essay about how wrong it is to pick on someone," she said.

"Except me, right?" Trina asked.

"Even you, Trina."

"But they were making fun of me. Why do *I* have to write an essay?"

"For spreading rumours about Marty in the schoolyard this morning." Like Santa Claus, Ms. Hawkins knew who was naughty and who was nice.

"I don't have anything to write with," Trina said.

Ms. Hawkins gave her number two pencil to Trina, who frowned as if she had just found a lump of coal in her stocking.

"Everyone get started," said Ms. Hawkins.

Usually other people teased *me*, so I didn't know how it felt to be the bully. I could write about how I felt when kids laughed at me: I wanted to throw up. I wanted to cry. I wanted to yell. I wanted to crawl inside my chest and never come out. Would telling the kids how I felt make them stop, or would it make them want to pick on me more?

I put my pen down and looked around the class. Ms. Hawkins was typing at her computer while the students were writing their essays. Who could be Graffiti Ghoul? Shane Baxter might have the nickname "Ghoul." He was a walking brick wall with a buzz cut. He picked on everyone, especially grade two kids. Every lunch hour he'd take their lunches, pick the best sandwiches for himself and stomp on the rest.

Even though he looked like a normal kid, he acted like a monster.

I whispered in Shane's direction, "Ghoul."

If Shane went by that nickname, he'd look up.

"Hey, Ghoul," I repeated.

He stared at his paper while he chewed his pencil stub.

"Ghoul," I said a little louder.

One desk past Shane, Trina looked up at the sound of my voice. She looked annoyed. I pretended to work on my essay, watching out of the corner of my eye until Trina went back to work.

"Ghoul," I coughed.

Shane didn't move. He was either deaf or he wasn't Ghoul. I was about to try one more time when Ms. Hawkins softly touched my shoulder.

"You should cover your mouth when you cough," she whispered.

I liked the fact that, even though she'd caught me talking in class, she made me stop without making me feel bad. I finished my essay, hoping that Remi would have better luck in finding Ghoul.

The news of the graffiti had spread quickly. Everyone wanted to see the message, but Mr. Henday had roped off the equipment shed. Kids crowded around the rope and craned their necks, but they couldn't see the shed doors or the graffiti.

Trina ordered, "Get back. Nothing to see here."

"Who died and made you queen?" Jacques Boissonault sneered.

Trina pointed to the orange sash that hung off her shoulder. It read: "Litter Patrol."

"*Hel-lo*," she said. "Talk to the sash."

At the start of the school year, Principal Henday asked for volunteers to work as Litter Patrol Officers to make sure the schoolyard stayed clean. The only person who volunteered was Trina. She got the job and the orange sash and the power went to her head.

"Now move along," she ordered everyone. "If you want something fun to do, you should go to the gas station and buy some slushies."

No one moved. I wandered behind kids, coughing, "Ghoul."

Jacques shot me a dirty look. "Cover your mouth when you cough. Were you raised in a barn?"

No one else reacted to my coughing.

Remi breezed past me and hissed, "Smelly feet."

"Smelly feet" was code for "Meet me at the Jesus statue." The stone figure stood on a tall pedestal, which put Jesus' feet at nose level and gave Remi the idea for the code phrase. He stayed on the French side of the statue while I leaned against the English side. No one could accuse either of us of Crossing The Line.

"There's no 'Ghoul' here," Remi said.

"Maybe he's ashamed of his nickname," I suggested.

"He could be a she. Girls can draw better than guys."

"Eric Johnson draws doodles better than anyone in my class," I pointed out.

"Either way, no one's answering to the nickname."

"I guess that means Graffiti Ghoul doesn't go to our school."

"Then why would he draw graffiti here?" Remi asked.

"Maybe he used to go here, and a teacher gave him bad marks," I guessed.

"Or he had three strikes."

"No one's ever had three strikes."

"So we're at a dead end," Remi said.

I shook my head. "No. We can find out *how* Graffiti Ghoul painted the message."

"There was a can of spray paint by the door. Right beside the broken beer bottle."

"I remember seeing that. Ghoul had to get the paint from somewhere. Where do you get spray paint?"

Remi's face screwed up like he was about to squeeze off a fart; this was his thinking look. I thought I'd better help him come up with the answer. I swung my arm up and down, pretending to hammer nails into a wall.

"What am I doing?" I asked.

"You're fishing? You're ringing a bell. No, you're the Pope and you're blessing a sheep."

"I'm using a hammer."

"Who cares about a hammer? We're trying to find a place to buy spray paint."

"It's a hint, Remi. The same place you'd get a hammer."

"Under my dad's pillow?"

"No. You get — wait a minute. Why does your dad keep a hammer under his pillow?"

"In case of burglars."

"Never mind," I said. "Listen. You get spray paint at a hardware store. That's where we have to start looking."

FOUR

Like my parents' store, Bouvier Lumber and Hardware was both a business and a home. The owner, Mrs. Gervais, lived in the apartment over the store with her thirty-year-old son, One-Eyed Pete. During the summer the two spent most of their waking hours in the store, helping customers pick out paint colours or find the right kind of screws. In autumn, business slowed down and Mrs. Gervais spent most of her time building birdhouses behind the store while One-Eyed Pete worked on his motorcycle. I hoped business was slow enough that one of them would remember who bought the spray paint.

Mrs. Gervais loved to decorate her store for Halloween. As Remi and I neared the store, I noticed cardboard skeletons taped to the plate glass window in awkward positions, as if they were trying to breakdance. In the window display cobwebs covered a bloodied ladder, a severed hand tried to crawl out of a half-opened toolbox and a human skull gripped a screwdriver as if it was a rose between its yellow teeth.

We went inside, stopping at a plastic Jack O' Lantern that overflowed with Mojos. Remi grabbed a handful and tossed me one of the pebble-hard candies. In the store, a teenager, dressed all in black except for a green apron and a silver-studded dog collar around his neck swept the floor. When he noticed us he rolled his eyes, swatted dust across the aisle with his straw broom and stomped away.

"What's his problem?" I whispered.

Remi shrugged. "My big sister's like that, too. Hey, tape's on sale. I need some for my hockey stick."

Remi picked up two rolls of black tape from the shelf beside us.

I shook my head. "Later. We've got a job to do."

He tossed the rolls of tape back on the shelf.

We circled the store, passing hacksaws, utility knives, bins of screws and trays of nails. Hardware supplies were pointy and dangerous. I wondered if One-Eyed Pete had lost his eye while he was stocking the shelves; maybe *that's* why he wore an eye patch. Finally we found the paint supplies near the back. We saw brushes, rollers, paint trays and big cans of paint, but found no cans of spray paint.

"Maybe Graffiti Ghoul bought it all," Remi said.

I nodded. "That means there's going to be more graffiti."

"Not if we can help it," Remi said. "Let's find out who bought the paint."

We looked around for Mrs. Gervais or One-Eyed Pete, but it looked like the sulking sweeper was the only person in the store.

"Excuse me," I called to him. "Can you help us?"

The guy stopped sweeping, sighed and shambled toward us. "Wadayawan," he mumbled, thanks to the silver stud pierced through his tongue.

"Can you help us?" I asked, peeking at the name tag on his green apron. "Patrick?"

"Wha do ya wan?" he said slowly.

"Do you sell spray paint?" I asked.

"We're ow."

"Are you hurt?" Remi asked.

"Wha?" Patrick looked puzzled.

"You said ow," Remi explained.

The guy shook his head. "Ow. We're ow. No more pain."

"If there's no pain, why are you saying ow?" I asked.

Patrick huffed and unscrewed the stud in his tongue. "I said we're out. No more *paint*. You under-standee Engleesh?" He glared at me.

"Who bought it?" Remi asked.

"None of your business. You gonna buy something or not?"

"If we do, will you tell us who got the paint?" I asked.

He growled, "If you buy something then I won't have a reason to throw you out of the store for loitering."

"I was going to buy some tape," Remi said.

"Oooo. Big spender," Patrick said.

Remi hustled to get the tape, leaving me alone with the cranky stock boy.

"I think you'll tell me who bought the paint," I said, crossing my arms and tapping my finger against my elbow. The trick worked for Principal Henday; maybe it would work for me too. I sucked wind through the gap between my front teeth, making a soft whistle as I tapped fast and furious.

"You got a problem?" Patrick grunted.

I tapped faster, trying to make him crack under the pressure of my stare.

Patrick lunged like he was going to punch me. I stumbled backwards, knocking some paintbrushes on to the floor.

Patrick laughed. "Nice move, Flinchie. Pick them up."

I did as he said, wondering why The Rake's trick didn't work on the teenager.

Remi returned with three rolls of tape. "How much for these?"

"Two forty," Patrick said.

Remi pulled out a quarter and a dime. "Uh, Marty, do you have any money?"

I shook my head.

Patrick grabbed the rolls of tape out of Remi's hands. "You two weirdos are wastin' my time. Get out."

"We'll get the money," Remi said.

"Out," Patrick ordered. He shoved us through the front door and slammed it shut behind us.

Remi glared at the store. "He's calling *us* weirdos? He should look in the mirror sometime."

"Never mind him. There's got to be another way to find out what happened to the spray paint," I said.

"What about Mrs. Gervais?" Remi suggested.

"Not a bad idea."

Behind the building, One-Eyed Pete's motorcycle sat beside Mrs. Gervais' work bench, where Mrs. Gervais was hammering a nail into the roof of one of her many unfinished birdhouses.

"Mrs. Gervais?" I said.

She looked up as she swung her hammer down on her thumb. "Ouch!" She dropped her hammer and sucked her thumb. "You shld snee uh on a psn ike at."

Remi said, "Uh . . . sorry?"

She pulled her thumb out and examined it. "That's okay. I wasn't planning on hitchhiking this week. What can I do you for, boys?"

"We're looking for spray paint," I said. "Patrick said you're sold out."

She shook sawdust out of her curly brown hair. "Not sold out, exactly. I'm not carrying it any more."

"Why?" Remi asked.

"Someone shoplifted all my cans of spray paint last week."

I remember the first time I spotted a shoplifter in my parents' store. A little boy tried to steal a Popsicle. He lifted his shirt and hid the Popsicle underneath, but he couldn't stand the icy bar against his skin and put it back. Graffiti Ghoul had to have a big shirt to steal all the cans of paint.

Mrs. Gervais picked up her hammer and said, "So I'm not carrying spray paint anymore. You'll have to go to Edmonton."

"Thanks, Mrs. Gervais," I said. "We'll do that."

As we walked away, One-Eyed Pete came down the stairs. He yawned, looking like he'd just crawled out of bed. He scratched the underside of his barbwire-tattooed arm and yelled, "Mom, we're out of potato chips."

"Are your legs broken?" Mrs. Gervais yelled. "Pick some up from the store."

"*You* do it," he ordered.

"What did you say?"

"I said you do it."

Mrs. Gervais grabbed her son in a headlock and smacked a bongo beat on his scalp with her palm.

"Ow. Mom. Stop. That hurts."

"What do you say?" Mrs. Gervais grunted, her hand poised for another smack.

"Sorry. I'm sorry."

"Sorry what?" Mrs. Gervais barked.

"I'm sorry, Mommy."

"That's better. And clean up that oil spill under your bike. And Pete, how many times do I have to tell you? Don't use my tools when you're working on the bike. You're a big boy now; you can use your own wrenches."

I thought only *my* mom embarrassed me in public. Maybe it was every mom's job to humiliate her son. I shuddered at the thought of what my mom would do to me when I reached One-Eyed Pete's age.

"Do you think Graffiti Ghoul stole the paint?" Remi asked as we walked away from the storefront.

I nodded. "This is turning out to be a real crime spree."

"Where do you think he'll hit next?"

"I don't know," I said.

As we neared the town library, I noticed the bush beside the building: it was shaking.

"I think he'll do the school next," Remi guessed. "With all the paint he has, I bet he's going to write a long message this time."

There was no wind. How could the bush move like that?

"Marty, did you hear me?"

The bush shook again; it looked like something, or someone, was behind it.

"Are you listening?"

I elbowed Remi in the ribs and whispered, "Someone's watching us."

FIVE

Remi squinted at the bush beside the library, stretching on his tip-toes to see behind it. I cuffed the back of his head.

"Ow. What did you do that for?"

Slowly and loudly, like I was talking to my hard-of-hearing grandmother, I said, "Remi, the sign says Bouvier Public Library."

"Why are you talking like that? Are we playing robots again?"

Out the side of my mouth I whispered, "Don't let them know we see them. Act natural."

Remi smacked the back of my head.

"Ow. What was that for?"

"That's what I'd normally do. Newton's Law," he said.

Remi based his code of justice on a science book I once showed him. A scientist named Isaac Newton came up with a law: for every action there had to be an equal and opposite reaction. If you kicked a ball, it would roll away from you with as much force as you kicked it with. A light tap didn't send the ball very far, while a hard kick would knock it across the soccer field. Remi thought Newton was talking about justice and dishing out punishment, because he had specifically used the word "law." If someone hit him, Remi reasoned, he'd have to punch back with just as much force.

"I told you before, it's not that kind of law," I said.

"Then why did he call it a law?"

"Never mind. Just keep walking."

Remi followed as I walked past the library.

"Who do you think is spying on us?" he whispered.

"I think Graffiti Ghoul knows we're on to him."

Remi glanced back at the bush. "Let's tackle him."

I spoke loudly and slowly so that our bush spy could hear. "No Remi. We have to go over our super secret plan in lots of detail."

"What plan?"

"The super secret plan." I cracked my neck to the left and then the right and yawned, covering my mouth with both hands. I hoped he'd pick up the signal.

Remi copied my ultra-slow way of talking: "Oh yeah. The super secret Ghoul plan."

I nodded toward the passageway between the library and the DVD rental shop next door.

"Let's go to my place and go over the plan," I shouted.

"That is a good idea," he yelled back. "Let's go now."

The bushes rustled. Our spy had taken the bait.

I yelled, "Now!"

I sprinted between the buildings. Remi ran right beside me, but the alley was only wide enough for one person. We became wedged against each other and the stucco walls.

"Move," I yelled.

"I'm stuck. *You* move."

"I can't."

"Turn to the side, Marty. Go thin."

I flattened my face against the library wall, squeezing myself thin so Remi could squirm forward until he popped free. He sprinted down the alley. I followed, brushing the stucco off my jacket as I ran. By the time I reached the back of the library, Remi had rounded the other corner and skidded to a stop. He waved me back.

"The spy's gone," Remi said. "I think he's run down the street. Cut him off."

I sprinted through the alley and zipped back to the front of the library. On my side of the street an old farmer climbed out of his pick-up truck, straightened his John Deere hat and walked into the hardware store. Across the street a mother pushed a baby stroller. Neither of them looked like the graffiti type, and there was no one else around. Our spy had vanished.

Remi joined me. "Did you see him?"

"No. He disappeared," I said.

"He must be really fast."

"Or he went inside." I nodded toward the library.

"You could be right, Marty."

"Let's get him," I said. We were close to catching the criminal — I was sure of it.

Remi bolted up the cement steps and opened the glass door for me. I sprinted into the library, but our town librarian, Mrs. Gibson, stopped me with a raised talon-like finger to her beak. On a stool behind a counter she perched like a vulture waiting to swoop on noisy prey. Remi rammed into my back.

"Get in there," Remi urged. "What's the holdup?"

Mrs. Gibson squawked, "Shhh."

Remi looked down at his feet, quiet as a mouse. We crept past the counter under Mrs. Gibson's beady-eyed gaze. At a table, three young girls huddled around a picture book with a unicorn on the cover. They didn't look like they could be spies. Brats, yes; spies, no.

"We should split up in case Graffiti Ghoul tries to get away," I whispered.

"Good idea," Remi replied. "What's the signal for when we find him?"

"Two whistles, five barks, and a — "

"Ahem." Mrs. Gibson shook her head, her brown hair standing up like ruffled feathers.

"Sorry, Mrs. Gibson," I whispered, then glanced at Remi and flapped my arms, miming a chicken.

He nodded and tiptoed toward the magazine area at the back of the library, while I stepped between two nearby bookcases. We weren't leaving until we caught our spy. I peeked through the shelves. In the next aisle, someone crouched at the far end of the book-shelf. Were they looking for books on the lower shelves, or were they hiding? Did they have a dust allergy and had to breathe hard, or were they panting from running? This could be our spy, I thought as I snuck forward. I got ready to tackle the spy, but the faint scent of strawberry bubble gum stopped me. I peeked around the corner and saw a girl with a blonde ponytail. This was no spy; this was Trina Brewster.

I had to get away before she saw me. Backing up, I bumped my elbow into the bookshelf. "Ow."

Trina swivelled around, holding a book in her lap. Her brow furrowed when she saw me.

"What are you doing here?" she whispered.

"Uh . . . I'm looking for a book," I stammered. I fumbled for a book on the shelf beside me, grabbed one and showed it to Trina.

She read the title, "*The Horsewoman's Passion.* What's it about?"

"Well, it's about a horse . . . woman. And her passion."

"Which is?"

"Horses?" I said.

"Are you following me?" Trina's lips curled into a cruel smile. "Wait till everyone at school hears about this."

She stood up, arming herself with a pointy insult, but Remi unknowingly stepped in front of her jab.

"Marty, I didn't find anyone," Remi said.

I said nothing, nodding my head toward Trina until Remi turned around and saw her.

"Are you guys here together?" Trina asked.

"No," Remi and I blurted.

Mrs. Gibson's hiss cut us off. We froze, expecting the librarian to swoop down and carry us off in her talons.

I lowered my voice. "Remi and I happened to be in the library at the same time."

Trina squinted at Remi. "Do you read?"

"Uh huh," he grunted.

"He had trouble looking for a book, so I told him I'd help," I explained.

Trina asked, "Remi, were you looking for the book that Marty has?"

"Uh . . . yeah," Remi said. "Thanks, Marty."

"So you read romance novels?" Trina asked.

"Romance what?" Remi said.

"Romance novels," I whispered.

Trina had fresh arrows for her gossip quiver. "So you're a lover, not a fighter."

I stumbled for an explanation. "He was getting it for his sister."

"Yeah. It's not for me," Remi said.

If Trina's smile grew any wider, it'd fly off her face. "Let me get this straight. You pick up mushy gooey romance novels for your sister?"

I tried to change the subject. "What book do *you* have?" I hoped Trina had something just as embarrassing.

She held up a book about Isaac Newton. "I'm doing a research project."

Remi whispered, "Hey, that's the same book Marty took out last month. You two like the same books."

"No we don't!" I protested.

"Figures you had this book. I thought I saw boogers on the Table of Contents page," Trina said.

Mrs. Gibson swooped down on the three of us. "How hard is it to keep quiet?"

"Sorry," we all said, but our apologies didn't quiet the ruffled librarian.

"This is a place where people come to read, not to socialize," Mrs. Gibson squawked. "You can chit-chat outside, but when you are in my library, you sit and you read and you zip your lips. You don't shout. You don't talk. You don't even whisper unless it's absolutely — "

"Shhhh," the three unicorn girls hissed from their reading table. "We're trying to read."

Mrs. Gibson shut her beak. She pointed at Remi and me, then motioned to the door.

"Why are you kicking *us* out?" Remi asked. "She was talking too."

Mrs. Gibson shushed him and pointed again. I nudged Remi out of the library.

Outside, Remi yelled, "You couldn't find a better book?!"

"Sorry."

"Now everyone's going to think I'm a sissy."

"Not after we catch Graffiti Ghoul," I promised.

"Well, he wasn't in there. I searched the library while you were having fun with Trina."

"It wasn't fun."

"Oh come on. You were acting like a monkey butt in love," he said.

The image of kissing Trina popped into my head. "Gross," I told Remi.

"You like Trina," Remi said.

"I do not!"

"You two can go read about Newton's laws together under that apple tree of his."

"I don't like her," I said.

"Relax. I'm just teasing," my friend said, chuckling.

"It's not funny."

"Sorry."

"I don't think Graffiti Ghoul went into the library," I said.

Remi nodded. "We'll have to catch him in the act."

"He'll probably be painting at night, when no one's watching," I said.

"How are we going to catch him then?" Remi asked.

"We have to go on a stakeout. Well, more like a *wander* out."

"My parents won't let me out at night," Remi grumbled.

"They will," I said, "on Halloween night."

SIX

Because Graffiti Ghoul was on to us, Remi and I needed to go undercover to catch the criminal, and that meant finding great Halloween costumes like the Spider-Man outfit that sat unsold on a dusty shelf in my parents' store. I wouldn't have a problem convincing my mom to let me wear it since she constantly used the things that didn't sell, from darning my socks with unsold needles to making sandwiches with stale bread.

In the kitchen, the smell of her cooking punched up my nose like dirty gym socks. Mom used alien ingredients she'd bought from a Chinese grocery store in Edmonton. A white turnip patty sizzled in a sesame-oiled wok. Brown soup with little red beans and pigeon meat stewed on the stove's back burner. On the kitchen counter, crimped eyelash bits of beef tripe waited to be added to the pot.

"Mom, can I wear the Spider-Man costume for Halloween?" I asked. "I don't think anyone's going to buy it."

She shook her head. "We can sell it next year if no one buys it."

"But I have to wear something for trick-or-treating."

Mom scooped up the tripe. "You not have to worry. I make you something to wear."

"Mom, that's too much work for you. I'll just borrow the Spider-Man costume. I want to look cool."

"Trust me. I picked your pants, didn't I?" She waved the tripe like a witch about to brew an evil potion. She tossed it into the hot soup. The tiny eyelashes shrivelled like my hope of wearing a decent disguise.

On Halloween night, Mom cackled when she showed me the costume. Before I could get away, she wrapped me mummy-like in the horrifying outfit. Then she pinned me down in a chair and poked my face with tiny crayons. I tried to see what Mom was doing to me, but she blocked the mirror while she tinkered with my face like a mad scientist. When she stepped back, and I saw myself in the glass, I wished I had never looked. I bolted out of Mom's "laboratory" and hid in the stockroom.

As I cowered in my hideous Halloween costume, I heard voices from the front of the store. My dad was talking to Remi.

"Marty! Your friends are waiting for you!" Dad's voice boomed.

Friends? I sneaked out of the storeroom and stole a peek. My detective partner had come with his big sister, Monique. Remi wore a long black trench coat and a pair of sunglasses. His brown hair was slicked back and he looked just like Neo from *The Matrix*. Not only did he have a good disguise, but he also looked really cool. Monique, on the other hand, wore the same denim jacket and pair of jeans that she wore whenever I saw her. She had the same "life sucks" eye-rolling expression as the dog-collared stock boy from Mrs. Gervais' hardware store. What happened on the way to high school that made teenagers permanently cranky?

"He's probably in the back," Dad told Remi. "Why don't you get him?"

"Hurry up," Monique said. "I don't have all night to babysit you two."

"Thanks, Mr. Chan," Remi said as he walked toward me.

I scrambled back into the stockroom and hid behind a tower of boxes. Why did I let Mom make my costume? Why didn't I tell her to put a sheet over my head and let me go as a ghost? I'd even go out in my fuzz-ugly corduroy pants.

"Marty?" Remi called out. "Are you ready for the wander out?"

Behind the boxes, I yelled, "Go without me. I'm not feeling so good."

He walked into the stockroom. "Marty, this might be our only chance to catch Graffiti Ghoul."

"I don't care what he does. I'm staying home. I look stupid."

"How bad can it be?" he asked. "Come out. I promise I won't make fun of you."

"Do you swear?"

"On my Wayne Gretzky hockey card."

"Okay," I stepped into the open. "What do you think?"

Remi lifted his sunglasses. His eyes popped wide open. A chuckle slipped past his lips. He tried to push it back in, but once the chuckle dribbled out, a stream of giggles followed. He clutched his belly and howled, unable to hold back the flood of laughter.

"You look like your mom," he said, gasping.

"You owe me your Wayne Gretzky card."

"Totally worth it," he wheezed. "What is that thing you're wearing?"

"It's called a Cheong Sam."

"It looks like one of your mom's dresses."

"It is."

Remi laughed even harder.

"Forget it. I'm not going," I said. The silky dress hung loosely on me like the wrinkly skin on a pug's face. The wig slipped over my eyes. As I pushed it back up I thought that Mom must have secretly wanted a daughter.

"This is the worst costume in the world," I sulked.

"Don't cry," Remi said, still laughing. "Your makeup will run."

"How'd *you* like to look like your mom?"

"No way!" Remi finally stopped laughing. "Hey, the good news is that no one's going to recognize you. It's a great disguise."

Monique called from the front of the store. "Are you guys coming?"

Remi yelled, "On our way!" He turned to me. "Think of this as going deep undercover."

"You sure no one will recognize me?"

"I'll bet your disguise will fool Monique," Remi said.

"She didn't know anyone named Ghoul, did she?"

"Nope. But she never tells me anything. Maybe she'd talk if you asked her. Let's go."

"Don't walk so fast," I said, stumbling after him in my mom's shoes. By the time I reached Monique, my feet were cramped and sore. How could Mom wear these cruel pink shoes? My toes barely fit into the pointy ends.

As soon as they spotted me, Monique and my dad burst out laughing.

"It's not funny," I said. The wig slipped over my eyes again. I fumbled with the fake hair, but the wig became tangled with my glasses and I couldn't take it off. Could this night get any worse?

FLASH! Mom had a camera.

"Move closer," she shouted. "I want to get a picture of you two together."

"No pictures," I yelled.

But Monique herded Remi and me together. FLASH! My Halloween nightmare would live forever in Mom's photo album right beside my naked-baby-bathing-in-a-kitchen-sink snapshot.

"Give Monique the camera so she can take more pictures," Dad suggested.

"We're going now," I said. I stumbled out the front door in the cramped pink shoes.

In the neighbourhood, ghosts haunted the streets while superheroes half-ran, half-flew down the sidewalks. Two elves sprang past me, firing fake arrows at a skinny orc. Everyone carried pillow cases or bags of candy. No one had a can of spray paint. Graffiti Ghoul wouldn't be in the open. He'd probably stick to dark alleys. I wished I owned a pair of infrared glasses, so I could see everything at night. At least this would make my glasses seem cool.

The first house Remi and I visited was a version of Disneyland's Haunted Mansion. On the lawn, a mannequin in a business suit tried to crawl out of a black coffin. Huge mutant pumpkins filled the yard, while curvy plastic snakes lined the front path. Tiny rubber spiders dangled from a giant web above the door.

"Trick or treat!" we yelled.

A pale vampire with a bowl of candy appeared at the screen door. "I vant to thuck your blood," he said.

"What?" I asked.

"I vant to thuck your blood," he said, drool dripping from his fangs.

"Is he speaking French?" I asked Remi, who shook his head.

Behind us, Monique translated the vampire's speech: "He wants to suck your blood. It's a line from a Dracula movie."

"Can we have our candy now?" Remi asked.

The vampire dipped his hand into the blood-splattered bowl and pulled out a lollipop. He dropped it into Remi's pillowcase.

"Vat about you, leetle girl," the vampire said to me. "Vat do you vant?"

Monique laughed. "He thinks you're a girl."

"I am not!"

He turned to Remi. "Ith thee your thithter?"

Remi looked at me, puzzled. "What?"

"Ith thee your thithter?"

Remi turned bright red. "My sister? No way."

Monique couldn't stop laughing.

Droolacula leaned forward and dropped two lollipops in my plastic shopping bag. "You get two lollipopth for being tho cute."

"Let me get a picture," Monique said.

I tried to scramble off the porch, but the vampire grabbed my arm and pulled me beside Remi. Close up, the vampire smelled like garlic and sweaty armpit.

FLASH!

"Got it!" Monique put away the camera.

That night every person who gave me candy called me a cute little girl. When I told them I was a boy, they chuckled and gave me more candy. I hated that it was so easy to mistake me for a girl.

Remi tried to cheer me up. "Hey, at least you're getting more candy than me."

I said nothing.

"Plus, no one recognizes you," Remi said. "It's a good disguise."

"*You* want to be a girl?" I growled.

"Duh. Do I look like a monkey butt?"

FLASH! Monique snapped another shot. When was she going to run out of film? We walked faster, hiding our faces from the camera.

"Did you see anyone who might be Graffiti Ghoul?" I asked.

"I didn't see anything suspicious."

Maybe we're on the wrong side of town." I shrugged.

"I heard that bad things happen on the other side of the railroad tracks," Remi said.

"How do you know which side is which?" I asked.

FLASH! Monique took another picture. "I'm going to blow that one up," she said. "One more for good luck."

I ran for cover, but there was no flash. Instead the camera whirred. The film was rewinding.

"At least things can't get any worse," I said.

"Think again." Remi pointed down the street.

Jean and Jacques Boissonault lumbered toward us.

SEVEN

"Why are they dressed like that?" Remi wondered.

The Boissonault brothers waddled down the street, dressed up to look like two giant slices of white bread. Their costumes were ridiculous, but bullies could wear whatever they wanted because no one would ever dare make fun of them.

"If they catch us Crossing The Line, we're in big trouble."

"It's okay. You're in disguise, Marty."

"Do you want to take a chance on getting nurpled?"

Remi slapped his hands over his chest. "Maybe you'd better hide."

I slid behind my friend and ducked low; he spread his jacket open like butterfly wings, shielding me from the approaching brothers.

"Your sister's catching up," I whispered. "She'll blow our cover."

Remi sped up, leaving me out in the open. I chased after him, crouching low. Suddenly he skidded to a halt and I did a face plant into the back of his trench coat, leaving some of my make-up on the back of his jacket.

"Hey, Remi. What's with the jacket?" Jean asked.

"Too hot," Remi said, still holding his jacket open. "I'm trying to cool off."

Jacques laughed. "You look like a dork."

I glanced through a hole in Remi's jacket. Jacques and Jean's bread costumes blew back and forth in the night breeze like floppy sails. Jean carried a slender can in his right hand but I couldn't read the label. Was he Graffiti Ghoul?

"Who's behind you?" Jean asked.

"What are you talking about?" Remi said.

Jacques pointed. "Turn around."

I squeezed tight against Remi's back as he shuffled around. My back bumped against a wooden gate, which creaked open. I jumped through the open gate and crouched behind the slatted fence.

"There's no one behind me," Remi said.

"She's right there," Jean said, pointing.

"Oh. That's just my sister."

Through a space in the fence I saw Monique join the boys. Jean dropped the can into his plastic Halloween bag. I had to get a closer look.

Monique asked Remi, "What's your friend doing?"

Jean said, "I'm not his friend."

"Don't look at me," Jacques said.

"Not you guys." Monique pointed at me. There was no other place to hide in the treeless yard. I was trapped.

"You mean . . . uh . . . Martina?" Remi said.

Monique snickered. "Yeah, *Martina*. I know she went into that yard."

"You hang out with a girl?" Jacques asked Remi.

"This I gotta see," Jean said.

The fence gate swung open, and Monique poked her head into the yard. "Let's go, *Martina*. No more games."

She held the gate open. I pulled the wig over my eyes, straightened up, and walked out. I stumbled in my heels on the sidewalk as the Boissonaults watched me.

I squeaked, "Nobody was home." I eyed Jean's trick-or-treat bag.

Jean whistled. "Hello."

Jacques elbowed his brother and stepped in front of me. "I'm Jacques."

"Hi!" I said, squeaking like Minnie Mouse.

Jean pulled his brother behind him. "I'm Jean, his better-looking brother."

Jacques shoved Jean aside. "Don't mind my idiot brother. He's got no manners. Say, have we met before?"

I shook my head and my wig almost fell off.

"You look familiar," Jean said.

"Yeah, you do. How do you know Remi?" Jacques asked.

Remi answered, "She's my cousin."

"I thought you said you were friends," Jacques said.

"She's my cousin and my friend," Remi said.

"Stop lying, Remi," Monique corrected her brother. "This isn't our cousin. It's — "

I cut Monique off: "I'm his girlfriend."

"What?!" Remi cried. "NO WAY!"

Monique laughed like a hyena, barely able to catch her breath. The Boissonault brothers looked puzzled. Remi, his face bright red, glared at me. I wanted to tell him that I had no choice; anything was better than being caught Crossing The Line. The sting of embarrassment was nothing compared to the pinching pain of ninety-nine nurples.

"We're not dating," Remi declared.

Monique laughed. "The lovers' first fight. Maybe you should kiss and make up."

Remi jumped away from me, squeezing between Jean and Jacques.

Jacques smirked. "I think someone's got cold feet."

Jean agreed. "Martina, if he won't kiss you, I will."

"I'm not that kind of girl," I said.

Monique howled, "You're telling me!"

Remi said, "Let's just go."

"Not yet," I said.

"Are you nuts?" Remi exclaimed, walking toward me.

Jacques grabbed the back of Remi's jacket. "That's no way to talk in front of ladies."

"It's okay," Monique said. "She's no lady."

Jean nudged Remi. "Tell Martina you're sorry."

"Sorry," Remi grumbled.

Jacques swatted the back of Remi's head. "Say it like you mean it."

"I'm sorry," Remi said, then shuffled out of swatting range.

"It's okay," I replied. "Actually, I'm feeling faint. Jean, do you have any food in your bag?"

Jean grinned. "What do you want?"

"Can I look?"

"He's got nothing. Look in *my* bag." Jacques shouldered his brother aside.

"She asked me first," Jean said.

"Why don't I look in both?" I asked.

The Boissonault brothers snapped open their bags. I only cared about what was inside Jean's bag — chocolate bars, Mojos, an apple, and the can. I pulled out the can.

Jean took it from me. "Silly. You can't eat this."

Remi craned his neck to see. "What's the can for?"

Jacques pulled out a similar can. "If people don't treat, we have to trick."

He popped the lid off and shot Silly String at Remi. Neither of the Boissonault brothers were Graffiti Ghoul, just bullies with canned string.

"I don't see anything I want to eat," I said.

The brothers' smiles dropped. Remi ushered me away. "Let's go, *Martina.*"

"Hey Jean, are you hungry?" Jacques asked, glaring at Remi.

Jean nodded, "I'm starving. What do you have to eat, Jacques?"

His twin brother smiled. "How about . . . a SAND-WICH?!"

The Boissonault brothers grabbed Remi and body-checked him, making him the filling between their slices of bread.

"Ugh. You guys stink!" Remi shouted.

"Jean, are you still hungry?"

"You bet. How about another . . . SANDWICH!" Jacques cried out as the two brothers gave my friend a second helping of their joke.

Remi staggered forward, barely hanging on to his pillow case of candy while the bullies laughed.

Jacques beamed. "Great idea for costumes, Jean."

Jean laughed. "I'm never going to get sick of that joke. See you later, Martina."

Jacques waved goodbye, and the brothers walked away, high fiving each other. Remi leaned against me, trying to catch his breath.

"Did you have to tell those snot gobblers you were my girlfriend?"

"Sorry, Remi," I said. "I thought I saw the 'you-know-what' and I thought the brothers were the 'you-know-who'."

Monique walked over. "Time to take *Martina* home."

But our wander out wasn't done yet. "I still want to do more trick-or-treating," I said.

"My pillow case isn't even half full," Remi whined.

"My mom said I could stay out for another hour," I said.

"You can come over to our place and count your candies," Monique said. "Now let's go. It's cold, and I've got homework to do."

Remi shook his head. "You're lying. You never do homework. You just want to get home so you can see your boyfriend before Mom and Dad come home from bingo."

"Shut up," Monique growled.

Remi smooched the air.

"Quit it," I said. "We need her so we can stay on the wander out."

He didn't hear me. He hugged himself and pretended to kiss an invisible partner. "Oh, Brian. You're so strong, but your hands are so soft," he said.

"You're going to get it when we get home," Monique said. "Now let's go."

She grabbed Remi by the collar, and dragged him down the street. Our wander out was a bust.

EIGHT

Monique led us through Bouvier's dark territory like a jungle explorer. We cut through backyards, squeezed through a broken section of a wooden fence and navigated unlit alleys until we reached Main Street. I'd never been to Remi's house, so I had to stick close to the Boudreaus or I'd get totally lost. We crossed Main Street and headed for the cul-de-sac between the church and my school. The fir trees, lined up like soldiers along a parade route, ran along a short road past the towering brick buildings to the squat Georges P. Vanier Composite High School. A chain-link fence surrounded the drab one-storey junior and senior high school building. The greyed venetian blinds in every window reminded me of cell bars.

"Quit gawking," barked Monique. "I don't have all night to wait for you goofs."

Now I knew why teenagers were always so cranky; I'd be upset too if I had to go to this prison school.

Remi started to climb the fence.

"Elementary students aren't allowed in the high school yard," I said.

One time, Eric Johnson tossed a Frisbee over the fence of the high school grounds. Instead of leaving it there, he climbed the fence to get it. A pack of teenagers caught him and tried to make him eat the Frisbee. When he couldn't bite through the plastic, the boys stuffed Eric into a garbage can and rolled him across the street back to our school. Since then, no elementary student ever went near Vanier.

"You're going to get in trouble," I said.

"It's night. There's no one here. We'll be safe."

"Are you sure?"

"I do it all the time," he said.

Monique was already at the top of the fence. "Come on."

"Okay . . . " I started to climb the fence. A chilly breeze blew up my skirt. I stepped back. "I can't."

"It's easy, Marty," Remi said. "Climb up and swing your leg over and jump down on the other side.

"I'll rip my mom's dress."

"Oh, right." Remi hopped down. "Monique. We're going the long way."

She landed on the other side. "I'm not climbing the fence again."

"We're almost home. Marty and I can make it the rest of the way by ourselves," Remi said.

"Yeah, and you'll tell Mom that I bailed on you."

"Then maybe she'll let me go out on my own."

Brother and sister glared at each other through the chain-link fence.

"This is stupid," Monique muttered. She climbed the fence and straddled the top. "Marty, let's go."

"My mom will kill me if I rip her dress."

"Don't be a baby," she said. "Give me your hand."

She reached down. I slowly raised my hand, thinking she was going to pull me up and over. Instead, she grabbed my sleeve. The silky Cheong Sam dress slipped right off me!

"Now you don't have to worry about ripping the dress," she said, holding it up.

"Give that back," I said.

"Ew! Skid mark." Remi pointed at my underwear. Monique chuckled.

"It's not funny," I said. "Give back the dress."

Remi yelled at his sister, "Just toss it down. Marty and I'll walk around the yard."

"Quiet," Monique hissed. "Someone's coming. It's the Sandwich Brothers."

Remi and I scrambled up and over the fence. I landed on the other side and laid flat on the cold, crunchy lawn beside Remi. I listened for the Boissonaults, but heard only Monique's laughter.

"Gotcha!" She said.

Remi stood up. "You dumb monkey butt."

His sister sneered. "I got your friend moving, didn't I?"

"Monique," I interrupted. "Can I have my dress back now?"

She tossed me the Cheong Sam. She hopped down off the fence while I pulled the dress over my head with Remi's help.

"You two look so cute. Like a married couple," she teased.

"Take that back," Remi said. "Or else."

"Or else what? You'll cry?"

He charged at his sister, but she neatly stepped aside and grabbed him in a headlock.

"Do you like that? Does it smell good?" Monique turned his head and rubbed his nose in her armpit.

"No. No. Ugh. It stinks. It stinks."

"Take a big whiff."

"Gross. Let go."

"Say uncle."

"No," Remi gagged.

"Say it."

She twisted him around again. I thought his head was going to pop off.

"Uncle," he finally grunted.

"Works every time," she said to me, letting go of her brother.

"Duh! Uncle doesn't count when my fingers are crossed."

"Sounds like someone needs another *pit* stop."

"I dare you," Remi said, stepping beyond her reach.

"Do we have to climb the fence again?" I asked, trying to change the subject.

Monique shook her head. "There's a gate on the other side. Let's go."

The frosty grass crunched under our feet like we were walking on shredded wheat. We headed along the front of the school building until we reached the track field. Across the wide yard, fir trees towered over the fence, marking the end of the schoolyard.

Behind her brother, Monique stepped on the back of his shoes, tripping him up.

"Quit it," Remi said, picking up the pace.

She hopped forward, snagging his other shoe.

He spun around. "I said quit it."

"Don't be a baby."

"You want to walk in front, go ahead."

"You first," Monique said.

Shivering in my thin Cheong Sam, I hoped the bickering Boudreaus would run out of steam soon, but as they walked ahead of me, I heard something else in the air. Distant laughter.

"Do you hear that?" I asked.

Monique turned around. "You think I'm going to fall for that gag?"

"I'm serious," I said. "Listen."

The laughter grew louder.

"Where's that coming from?" I asked.

"From behind the fir trees," she replied.

"What's there?" I asked.

Remi whispered, "The graveyard."

NINE

"Do you guys live next to the cemetery?" I wasn't sure if I wanted to hear the answer.

Remi looked down at his feet.

"Yes," Monique answered. "We do."

"Is that why you never invite me to your house?" I asked Remi.

A shrill wail from the graveyard cut off his answer.

"Who's screaming?" Monique asked.

The track field that separated us from the cemetery seemed to shrink before my eyes like a collapsing telescope.

"I don't know," I said. "I don't think I want to find out."

She shushed me. "Listen."

Out of the darkness a girl screamed. Laughter floated out from the cemetery, over the chain-link fence and across the track field toward us. I wished I was home in bed under my covers. I inched closer to Remi.

"Maybe we should leave them alone," I suggested.

"Are you two scared?" Monique asked.

Remi pushed me away. "No. Marty's the one who's trying to hide behind me."

"You're the one who's shaking," I said.

"What's that? I can't hear you. Your knees are knocking too loudly."

"You're scared too," I accused.

"I'm rubber, you're glue. Whatever you say bounces off me and sticks to you," Remi said.

"You're a big chicken."

"Boing. Right back at you. Bwock, Bwock," Remi clucked.

I'd have to remember Remi's neat trick the next time someone insulted me.

"You two are goofs," Monique sighed.

"We're rubber, you're glue," I said. "Boing!"

Remi nodded approval.

Monique whispered. "If you two knew who's in the cemetery, you wouldn't be playing stupid games."

"What are you talking about?" I asked.

"Who's there?" Remi leaned forward.

"Is it someone we know?"

Monique shook her head. "It's no one you want to know."

My stomach twisted into a pretzel, but Remi shrugged, unafraid.

He confronted his sister: "You're lying. You don't know who's in the graveyard. You don't even — "

Low moans cut him off. Now the cemetery sounded like a restaurant full of cows that ate way too much off the buffet table.

"You guys ever hear of The Curse of Bouvier Cemetery?" she asked.

I shook my head and scanned Remi's puzzled face for a clue. He shrugged.

"Do you want to hear it?" she asked.

I was pretty sure she meant to tell us the story whether we wanted to hear it or not. The way she asked reminded me of how my grade three teacher, Mrs. Connor, used to ask Eric Johnson if he "wanted" to re-do his homework, or how my mom asked if I "wanted" to take out the garbage. Why did they even bother asking?

Sure enough, Monique launched into her tale before Remi and I could say a thing: "When I started grade seven at Vanier, there was a gang that ruled the school — the Gangstas. These guys were serious trouble and they knew it. They skipped classes. They stuffed nerds in lockers. They clogged toilets with pages from textbooks. They even lipped off the principal."

"What's 'lipped off' mean?" I asked.

"They talked back to him," she said.

"Why did they do that?" he asked.

"Because they felt like it. They did anything they wanted. They drank beer. They threw parties on the roof of the school. They stole the wheels off cars."

"Couldn't anyone stop them?" Remi asked.

She shook her head. "Everyone was afraid. The Gangstas held grudges. I heard that a grade twelve girl told them to stop being jerks and the next year, she never came back to school."

"Maybe she graduated," I suggested.

Monique shook her head. "She was supposed to come back and finish math and chemistry. Rumour is that the Gangstas made her disappear for what she said to them."

"Are they still around?" Remi asked.

She silently looked toward the cemetery.

I asked, "What happened to them?"

"One night they went too far." Her voice grew soft. "They stole a car and went for a joy ride, down the road over there."

She pointed to the old highway which ran alongside the track field and past the cemetery.

She continued, almost whispering: "It was raining that night, and the road was slippery. They were going too fast and the car skidded off the road and into the cemetery. It rolled twenty-three times and landed in the middle of the graveyard. The Gangstas died. People say that the Gangstas were thrown out of the car so hard that their bodies went right into the ground, so when it came time to bury them, the undertakers just had to cover up the holes with dirt."

"What happened after that?" Remi squeaked. If there was a chair there, he'd be sitting on the edge of it.

"Weird noises started to come from the graveyard. The sound of moaning, laughing, and sometimes a scream. People said it was the Gangstas."

"But they were dead," I said. "Did they become ghosts?"

She said nothing.

Remi scoffed. "You're making this up. Someone must have checked out the cemetery and found something."

"A policeman did, but he never came back. He disappeared like the grade twelve girl. The police sent twenty men to the cemetery to look for the cop, but all they found was his chewed-up shoe. They say the Gangstas ate him, from head . . . to foot."

"Ghosts can't eat people," I said.

"I didn't say they were ghosts," Monique said. "The Gangstas became zombies. The undead. The creatures that feed on human flesh. They're going to eat your feet if you're not careful."

She advanced toward Remi and me.

He laughed. "You're just saying that to scare us."

"They're coming to get yo-o-o-u, Remi," she moaned.

"You'll have to do better than that."

Monique continued, "The graveyard ghouls are going to eat your toes first, then your foot and — "

I didn't hear anything else she said. Ghouls! My entire body went numb as the truth plopped in front of me like a pop quiz. The dead were rising from their graves to paint graffiti.

TEN

"Ghoul" wasn't a nickname; it referred to what our graffiti artist was — an actual ghoul. I had to tell Remi, but he was covering his ears to shut out Monique's moans. She kept pestering him as we left the schoolyard, claiming the ghouls were going to eat him.

"Are you done yet?" Remi asked his sister.

"Admit it. My story freaked you out or else you wouldn't be covering your ears."

He dropped his hands. "My ears are cold, that's all. Besides, why should I believe you?"

"Because it's the truth," Monique said.

"Sure," he scoffed. "Like you told the truth when you told Dad your watch died and that's why you missed curfew."

"My watch did break," she said.

"Did *Brian* fix it for you? Or was he too busy sucking the tongue out of your mouth?"

"Shut your trap," Monique said.

He smiled. "I think *he's* the zombie, the way he was chewing on your ear."

She smacked him in the arm.

"Didn't hurt," Remi said.

Monique shoved him aside and walked away, passing a green sign that read:

FOREST HEIGHTS ESTATES

"Is she crazy?" I asked. "She's heading into the trailer park. Don't you know who lives there?"

"Yeah. *I* live there," he said.

"Oh," I mumbled. "Sorry."

I shouldn't have called Remi's neighbourhood "the trailer park." To be fair, everyone called it that because it was, well, a park full of trailers. The long, narrow trailers were parked at angles so they could be towed out without hitting the houses across the lane.

"You don't have to come over," he grumbled.

"I want to," I said, wondering if Lawrence Bennet's claim that only criminals lived in the trailer park was true.

"You're not going to make fun of where I live, are you?"

"I wouldn't do that."

"Everyone else does," he said.

Teasing was like the flu; it made me feel like throwing up. The kids picked on me because I looked different, because I was Chinese, because I didn't fit in, but Remi looked the same as everyone else. I thought he'd be immune to the disease I called *teasitus*, but there must've been more than one way to catch this awful sickness. If Remi could come down with *teasitus*, then anyone could.

"Living in Forest Heights Estates isn't so bad," I said, trying to cheer up my friend. "At least you don't live in a grocery store."

He looked puzzled. "What's so rough about that? You get free candy whenever you want."

"I wish. Dad says candy's for paying customers. For snacks Mom sticks head cheese on crackers because it's the only meat that no customer will buy."

"What's head cheese?"

"Lunch meat that looks like it's been sliced from a cow's head."

"Gross."

"Plus, because the store is so gigantic, it takes me two hours to do my chores. Do you know how many trips I have to make to the dumpster? I'd live in Forest Heights Estates any day."

"Do you want to trade places?" Remi asked.

"Sure, you can let my mom dress you up in her clothes."

"Never mind."

"Are you going to invite me in your house? I'm freezing in this dress."

He chuckled, seeming more like his old self, and walked past a windmill mail box toward his trailer.

Remi's house reminded me of my home. All the rooms ran in a straight line like the back hallway of my parents' store. The difference was that his home had carpets, while mine had cement floors, and he had a bratty big sister, while I had none.

"Watch out for the ghouls," she moaned.

Remi led me along the wood-panelled hallway into his bedroom and shut the door, blocking out his sister's moans.

Finally I could tell him about my theory. "I think one of the Gangstas is drawing the graffiti."

"You can't be serious," he said. "You think we're dealing with a spray-painting zombie?"

He opened the top drawer of his dresser and dumped his candy into it. A hockey trophy tumbled off the dresser and landed in an unzipped hockey bag. By the time he fished the trophy out, a jockstrap had hooked around the tiny golden hockey player. He untangled it and flicked the jockstrap on to his messy bed.

"It's someone from the Gangstas," I said. I grabbed a hockey stick propped against a Wayne Gretzky poster, knocked the jockstrap off Remi's bed and sat down with the stick on my lap. "I think Monique's story is real."

"My sister always lies. Last week, she told my dad she was late coming home because there was a grease fire at her job and she had to clean the grill. But I saw her necking with her boyfriend in his car for like an hour outside the house before she came in."

"What's necking?" I asked.

He wrapped his arms around himself and smooched the air.

"Ew," I said, shuddering at this one-sided wrestling match.

Remi lowered his arms. "You can't trust anything that snot gobbler tells you."

"How do you explain what we heard from the cemetery?"

"It doesn't have to be ghouls," he said.

"Who else has a good time in a graveyard?" I asked. "Think about it. Halloween is party time for zombies, and the cemetery is like their community hall. They're probably bobbing for feet right now."

Remi scrunched his face and squeezed his eyebrows together. He was either thinking hard or he needed to fart. "If it was one of the Gangstas, the graffiti should have said 'Gangstas Rule', but it said 'Ghoul Rule'."

"Didn't Monique say that the Gangstas drank beer?"

"Yeah. So?"

"Don't you remember what was at the school shed? Under the message?"

His farty-thinking face returned. I hoped he was thinking.

"A beer bottle," I said. "It had to be from one of the Gangstas. What other proof do you need?

His face was still in fart-or-thinking mode. A slow trumpet toot was followed by the reek of rotten eggs. Nope, he wasn't thinking.

"Ooops," Remi said.

"Something crawled up you and died." I fanned the stink away from me.

"Beans," he said.

THUMP.

"What was that?" I asked.

THUMP. THUMP. Something was banging against the bedroom window.

"Someone's trying to get in." I stood up, clutching the hockey stick. "It's the Gangsta Ghouls!"

"Don't be silly," Remi said. "There are no such things as zombies."

He picked up his jockstrap and stretched it out like a slingshot.

"I thought you didn't believe in zombies," I said.

"Just in case."

"Ooooooohhhhhhhhhhmmmmmmmmm," a low voice moaned from outside the window.

My hands shook. "It's the undead."

He took aim at the window. "No it's not."

"The ghouls are coming to feed on us," I said.

"Chill!"

"We're going to be zombie dessert!" I cried.

Remi elbowed me, then yelled at the window, "Monique! I know it's you."

Of course! The moaning creature outside had to be his sister.

"Yeah," I added. "Stop joking around. It's not funny."

"I smeeeeelllllll feeeeeeeeet." The voice didn't sound much like Monique at all.

"Are you sure it's her?" I asked.

Remi nodded, then stared at the window. He didn't look very sure of himself.

"Feeeeeeeeeeeeeeeeet tooooooo eeaaaaaatttt," moaned the voice.

It had to be his sister, and if it was, then she needed a little dose of Newton's Law. Nudging my friend, I whispered, "Let's lock her out of the house."

He grinned. "That's why you're the brains and I'm the brawn."

I threw down the hockey stick, scrambled to the door and pulled it open. Monique jumped around the corner of the hallway and screamed, "Gotcha!"

I let out a high-pitched scream and hopped back. Remi fired his jockstrap, which smacked Monique in the face.

"You morons," she growled as she peeled the jockstrap off her head.

"There's a zombie outside," I said.

"And it's going to eat us," Remi said.

Monique smiled. "I thought you didn't believe in zombies, Remi."

"I'm telling the truth," he said.

"Yeah, right," she said.

"He is," I said, backing Remi up. "It's outside the window."

She cackled. "Maybe we should let it in." She walked to the window.

"What are you doing?" I cried. "Get away from there!"

"Don't open the window!" he yelled.

Too late. She slid the window open and looked out.

"There's no one out here," she said.

"Really?" I asked.

"See for yourself," she said.

Remi crept to the window. I stayed back. Monique stepped away from the window so her brother could peek out. Suddenly, a hand shot into the room, reaching for Remi. He screamed, but Monique held him by the arms.

"Feeding time," she yelled.

"No!" I screamed.

"Let go of me!" he screeched.

A burly blond guy in a Bouvier Bobcats hockey jacket appeared in the window.

"Gotcha again!" Monique let go of her brother.

Remi blushed. "I knew it was you, Brian."

"Is that why you were screaming like a girl?" Brian laughed. "I wish I coulda seen the look on your face when I was banging on the window."

"There's a zombie outside my window!" Monique mocked us. "Call mommy and daddy. I think I wet my pants!"

Brian pretended to be a hysterical Remi by running back and forth past the window, his blond hair flapping up and down like a dolphin's tail.

"Dad said you're not allowed to have friends over tonight," Remi said to Monique. "Especially not Brian."

Brian stopped and popped his head through the opened window. "Relax, runt. Monique asked me to drive your friend home."

"I don't need a ride," I said. I didn't want to go anywhere with this jerk.

"Do you want to walk instead?" Monique taunted. "Past the cemetery?"

Remi said, "I'll walk with him."

"Past the ghouls?" Brian asked. "Oohhhhhmm."

Between zombies and jerks, I didn't have much of a choice. "It's getting cold out there," I said. "Let's *all* go for a ride."

Monique shook her head. "Remi's gotta go to bed. School tomorrow."

"You can't leave me alone," he argued.

"We'll be back in twenty minutes," Brian promised. "It doesn't take that long to get to Marty's place."

Monique smiled. "Are you scared?"

If Remi rode with us, he'd be admitting that he was too scared to stay at home alone, and Monique would tease him for the rest of his life. But if he stayed at home, Monique and Brian would probably try to frighten him when they got back, and the only thing worse than being scared was waiting to be scared. My friend's problem was like a Jenga game; any block he pulled out would bring down the tower.

I had to save him. "I'll be okay. When your parents come back from bingo, you can tell them what Monique did."

Remi grinned. "Yeah, I'll tell them everything you did, Monique."

"Go ahead," she dared.

"And what you're going to do with Brian," he added.

She glared at him. "Marty, get your stuff. Brian will take you home now."

"I have to wash my face first," I said. "Or my mom will kill me."

Brian smiled. "Take your time. Monique, you want to keep me company until the kid's ready to go?"

She beamed. "Why don't we warm up the truck?"

Brian left the window and Monique hurried out of the bedroom. Remi ran to the window and slammed it shut.

"Do you believe the zombie story now?" I asked.

"I still need proof," he said.

"What kind of proof?" I wasn't sure I wanted to hear the answer.

"We have to check out the graveyard."

I shivered, and it wasn't from the cold.

ELEVEN

Remi and I had agreed to investigate the cemetery after school, but the thought of what we might find distracted me all day; zombies kept popping into my head. At lunch time, Samantha McNally took a sip from Trina's slushie and suffered a brain freeze that made her moan like a *zombie*. The Boissonault brothers replayed their sandwich joke, which seemed kind of stale without the costumes, on a French boy, and he stumbled in a daze through the yard just like a *ghoul*. In class, Ms. Hawkins talked about stories having two sides and the truth standing someplace between them, but all I heard was that *the undead* stood on both sides of me.

When the last bell of the day finally rang, I headed to my locker and pretended to organise my books, waiting for the kids to clear out. Then I grabbed a brown paper bag, checked its contents and headed off. As my footsteps echoed on the floor, I had the creepy feeling that zombies were watching me.

At the shed, Remi was waiting impatiently. "What took you so long?"

I held up my bag. "I had to get protection against the zombies."

"We're not even sure they're zombies," Remi said.

"In case they are . . . " I reached into the paper bag. "Vampires don't like garlic. The same should work on ghouls."

I pulled out a spice bottle of garlic powder.

"It could save us from being eaten," I said.

"Do you have one for me?" Remi asked. "In case you're right."

I pulled another spice bottle from the paper bag and tossed it to Remi.

He shook the glass bottle. "It's oregano," he said.

"It's all I could find. Don't worry, I mixed some garlic powder in with it."

My partner unscrewed the orange cap of his bottle and sniffed the contents while I folded up the bag and stuffed it in my back pocket.

"How much did you put in there?" he asked. "I can't smell any garlic."

"There should be enough."

"What if you're wrong?"

"Then run really, really fast," I said.

"Okay." He pocketed the spice bottle. "We're going to have to cut through the high school grounds."

"In broad daylight?" I asked.

"It's the only way to get to the cemetery. We can't walk along the highway."

"How about we cut across the field between your house and the cemetery?"

"If my mom spots me," said Remi, "she'll make me clean up my room, and we won't be able to get to the cemetery before dark. Don't worry. Teenagers don't stay at school longer than they have to. Everyone should be gone by now."

He was almost right. The school looked pretty empty. Five cars sat in the parking lot, but no people were hanging around the yard. Remi and I climbed over the fence and flopped on the grass.

"Okay, on my signal, we do six forward rolls to the school and then maintain the position against the wall."

"Why don't we just run?" I asked.

"I'm the commander of this mission," Remi said. "You do what I say."

"Okay, okay."

We rolled across the lawn. After the second roll, I lost control of where I was going and my momentum picked up until the sky and grass became one big blur, and SPLAT! My hands and face smacked into the school's brick wall. Remi smirked.

"Nice rolling," he teased, dusting the grass off me.

"Do I have a bleeding nose?"

"No, you're okay," he said. "But was your nose always that flat?"

I rubbed my nose, panicking, but Remi chuckled. "Kidding," he said.

"I knew that," I lied.

He peeked around the corner, then signalled for me to follow. We slipped around the corner and inched along the front of the school as if we were on the ledge of a high-rise building, ducking out of sight under the windows. But we couldn't duck under the all-glass doors of the main foyer.

"Move fast," he whispered.

He rolled across the pavement; I sprinted past him and waited on the other side of the doors. Remi rolled right into me, his head smacking into my special place, the one spot no one is ever supposed to hit. I doubled over while he flopped back on his butt. I grunted, trying to shake off the pain. I opened my mouth to scream, but Remi clamped his hand over it.

"Shhh. No noise. Just take deep breaths and don't think about the pain."

How was I supposed to ignore pain that hurt a million times worse than a nurple?

"Don't worry," he whispered. "The pain will go away if you breathe slowly."

Taking his advice, I breathed through my nose. My friend's hand smelled of grass and sweat. I pushed it away and walked off the pain.

"You okay now?" Remi asked. "Do you need to lie down?"

"Forget it. I'm good. Let's just go." I walked until I reached the far end of the school, where only the track field stood between us and the graveyard.

"How are we going to get across without anyone seeing us?" I asked.

"We can commando crawl on our bellies," he suggested.

"Where do you come up with these weird ideas?"

"My dad likes to watch war movies."

"I'm not crawling," I said.

"Okay, you can run, but zigzag a lot."

"Can't we just walk?" I asked. "No one's here."

"Hink ahin," a voice sounded from over my shoulder.

Patrick, the spiky-haired stock boy from the hardware store, stood behind us, his tongue stud still making him hard to understand.

"What did you say?" I asked.

Patrick unscrewed his tongue stud. "I said, think again."

Beside him a beefy boy in a jean jacket snickered, while a guy as tall as a basketball net laughed like a donkey. Just behind them, a girl with long, straight, jet-black hair crossed her arms and sneered. Her entire face was pale except for her black lips. She looked like someone had fed her black licorice until she got sick.

"You boys lost?" she asked. "You're a long way from Chinatown." She squinted at me, pretending to be Chinese.

"We're taking a shortcut to my place," Remi said.

"Yeah right." The beefy boy hawked a loogie on the ground.

"Watch where you're spitting, Dough Boy," warned the white-faced girl. She checked her black army boot for saliva.

"It's a free country, Snake Girl."

The skinny goon slapped his thigh and hee-hawed. "Good one. If anyone looks like a freak, it's Beth."

Patrick whacked him in the stomach. "Shut it, Warren." Then he stepped toward my friend. "You live in the cemetery? Because that's where it looked like you were headed."

Remi said nothing.

"I bet he's a T.P. punk," Beth said.

"Is that right, kid?" Dough Boy asked Remi. "Do you live in the trailer park? Do you live in a 'man-you-fractured' home?"

Warren hee-hawed, "You should call them T.P. Punk and Chinatown."

"You read too many comics," said Beth.

"You spend too much time in your coffin," Warren shot back.

"That's so funny I forgot to laugh," she said.

Patrick interrupted the bickering, warning Remi and me: "You brats know only high-schoolers are allowed here."

"We didn't know," I lied, hoping they'd let us off the hook.

"Hey, Chinatown, you know what happens to punks we catch on our grounds?" Dough Boy asked.

I clammed up. I knew exactly what happened. I scanned the schoolyard for garbage cans.

"What's the matter, Chinatown? Cat got your tongue?" Dough Boy said.

Warren disagreed. "It's the other way around. My brother says they eat cats."

Was Warren's brother the one who spread that awful rumour at my school? I wanted to tell him that his brother was wrong.

Dough Boy strolled toward me, "That true, Chinatown? You got a little meow-meow in your tum-tum? I'll bet your old man makes cat stew. That's why your store always stinks."

My stomach twisted into a knot, and I felt like throwing up. Another case of *teasitus*, and I had it bad this time.

Dough Boy sniffed me. "Smells like kitty."

"Leave him alone," Remi warned. "He didn't do anything to you."

Beth stepped in front of my friend. "Trespassing *and* talking back. Tsk. Tsk."

"You punks're in deep trouble," Patrick said.

Warren's mule snicker cut through the air. "What do you want to do to them?"

The four teenagers surrounded us.

Beth said, "Let's start with atomic wedgies."

"Hang them from the soccer net," Dough Boy suggested.

"Give them pink belly," Warren said.

Beth added, "Nurples."

"Hurts Donut," Dough Boy said.

Warren yelled, "Wet willies!"

"I say we do it all," Patrick said.

Patrick and Beth grabbed me while Dough Boy and Warren roughed up Remi. Dough Boy grabbed a fistful of the back of my friend's underwear and yanked until Remi yelped. Meanwhile, Beth stuck her index finger in her mouth and pulled it out slowly. A string of saliva hung on her fingernail. I squirmed backwards, but Patrick held me. Beth waved her sticky finger in front of my face. I squirmed and twisted my head away. She waved her wet-willying finger so close to my face I could see that the rings on her hand were shaped like snakes.

"You guys have a problem?" The voice belonged to Monique.

Everyone turned.

Her arms crossed, Remi's big sister glared at the goons. "No one picks on my brother," Monique said.

Dough Boy laughed. "This punk's related to you?"

"Let them go," Monique warned. "Or else."

"I can take care of myself," Remi said.

"Yeah, and you're doing a bangup job of it," sniped Monique. "It's a good thing I saw you two dorks sneaking around. You should know better."

"Maybe this will remind him." Dough Boy punched Remi in the arm. "Hurts, donut?"

Remi glared at Dough Boy but said nothing.

"Don't do that again," Monique ordered.

"Who's gonna stop me?" Dough Boy taunted.

"My boyfriend Brian is supposed to pick me up any minute." She flicked her long brown hair and glanced back at the street alongside the schoolyard.

"So?" Warren said.

"He's probably coming with his hockey buddies. You remember the Bouvier Bobcats. Most penalty minutes for fighting."

Patrick let go of me. Warren and Dough Boy glanced toward the street nervously. Only Beth didn't seem fazed.

"The punks learned their lesson," Patrick said. "Let's go before they start bawling."

He headed past Monique toward a blue car in the parking lot. Dough Boy and Warren let go of Remi and followed. The last to move, Beth sauntered toward Monique and bumped into her.

"You might want to lose some weight. I feel like a space ship in orbit around Uranus."

"I see you're still buying your accessories at the pet store," Monique said.

The pale girl's face reddened, but she recovered. She lifted her snake rings to her ear and pretended to listen to them.

"Do you know what they're saying?" Beth asked.

Monique shook her head.

"They're telling you to bite me."

"Why don't you slither back under the rock you came from?"

Snake Girl walked away, joining the guys as they climbed into a rusty blue two-door car. They sat in it, watching us.

Monique walked over to Remi. "Are you okay?"

"Yeah," he said, plucking at the seat of his pants.

"Good," she said. She punched his arm.

"Ow. What was that for?"

"That's for making me stand up for you. Now go home."

A horn honked. Brian's pick-up truck pulled into the parking lot. The truck's box was full of the Bouvier Bobcats, the town's hockey champions. Patrick and his gang drove out of the lot while Monique walked toward Brian's truck.

Remi whispered, "This is our chance to get into the graveyard." He sprinted across the track field toward the cemetery.

I followed him to the chain-link fence and row of fir trees that separated the track field from the grave-yard. Even in broad daylight the cemetery looked creepy. The trees blocked out most of the light and the pine needles killed most of the grass. The tomb-stones looked like stubby fingers clawing out of the ground.

We climbed over the fence and landed next to a patch of prickly bushes. Most of the yellow leaves had either fallen off or were about to. A few yellow leaves attached themselves to the back of Remi's jean jacket, but he didn't stop to brush them off. He crept along a row of tombstones. Some were short and black, others were tall and grey and one section had plaques for a bunch of nuns who all died in the same year, 1918. I walked behind Remi, taking the time to read each marker. The inscriptions were in English and French — either "Rest in Peace" or "Au Revoir." The English were buried next to the French. There were no divisions like there were at my school. Maybe only the living cared about Crossing The Line.

Then I spotted a marker that stopped my heart. On the squat stone base of a tall tombstone, an inscription read:

ALIVE

I whispered, "Someone's buried alive under there. I think I can hear them thumping against their coffin, trying to get out. It's horrible, terrifying, gruesome."

"Duh! It says 'Auve.' That's my great aunt's tombstone."

"Are you sure? It looks like it says 'alive'."

"Positive." Remi knelt down and wiped dirt that had collected on the bottom of the 'U'. The inscription now read:

AUVE

I breathed a sigh of relief. He crawled past the marker to the other row and picked up a beer bottle.

"Whoa." He let out a low whistle. "Jackpot."

Several beer bottles littered the patchy lawn around the tombstone.

"Whose marker is this?" he asked. "It might be a clue."

I read the tombstone: "Dylan Green. Loving son and brother. Survived by parents Hank and Anne and sister Elizabeth." The date was recent. "This guy died two years ago. He might be one of the Gangsta ghouls. That's why the beer bottles are here."

"That's not proof that they're drawing graffiti," Remi said, sounding unsure.

A glint from the ground caught my eye. A metal can partly covered by wilting flowers sat beside a tombstone. I picked up the slender can. Black spray paint.

"Graffiti Ghoul was here!" I said.

Remi looked at the can. "You might be right, but why is he painting graffiti?"

Snap.

"Was that you?" I asked.

Remi shook his head and pointed behind me. "It came from over there."

Four rows away, a shadowy figure ducked behind a tombstone.

TWELVE

"Garlic!" I yelled as I fumbled with the cap of my spice bottle. "Get the garlic!"

Faster than a gunslinger, Remi drew his spice bottle from his pocket, uncapped it, and shook it furiously over his hand. Nothing came out.

"It's clumping!" he yelled.

"My cap's stuck."

"Turn the other way."

I spun on my toes to the left. "This way?"

"No. Turn the *cap* the other way," he said.

Finally, the cap popped open. All the garlic powder spilled out, leaving only a dash of zombie protection.

"I'm out," I said.

"You had the full bottle."

"The powder's on the ground."

"Scoop it up!"

I dropped to the ground, sweeping the grass for garlic but finding only dirt.

"It's blown away," I yelled. "Run!"

Instead, my friend waved his clogged bottle of oregano/garlic in the air and advanced toward the tombstone: "Get back, creature of the undead!"

"Don't use it like that," I ordered. "Throw it like a grenade!"

Remi nodded and lobbed the bottle high in the air. Trina Brewster stood up from behind the tombstone and caught the bottle like an outfielder snagging a pop fly.

"Just what are you two doing?" she asked, examining the bottle.

"Trina?" I said.

"You guys said something about garlic and grenades?"

"I just farted," I lied.

"Yeah, gas grenade," Remi said. "Silent but deadly."

"Smelled like garlic," I added.

"Why are you here?" she asked. "Don't tell me. Marty, you're helping Remi find a tombstone for his sister to read."

I stammered for an answer. "Well . . . it's like . . . Remi . . . he . . . I . . . "

"You wanted to cook something?" Trina waved the spice bottle.

"Why are *you* here?" Remi went on the attack. "Are you following Marty again?"

"*Hel-lo*," she said snarkily. "I'm visiting my grandmother's grave."

"Where is it?" he asked.

"Over there," Trina waved to the other side of the cemetery.

"Show us," I said.

She scratched at her arm nervously and stuttered, "I-i-it's over there somewhere. M-my mom is the one who always brings me here. I-I never paid attention. I think I'm lost. All the tombstones look alike."

Sure that she was lying, I cornered her. "Maybe we can help you look."

She glared at me. "I don't need your help. If you don't mind, I have to pay my respects."

She spun around and walked away. The back of her hair was covered with tiny yellow leaves — the same ones from the prickly bushes.

"Wait a minute," I cried out. "You have leaves in your hair."

She brushed her head and shook out her hair. "So what?"

"Were you hiding in the bushes by the fence?"

"No." She fidgeted, shifting from one foot to the other, looking like she had something to hide.

I decided to lay out a trap. "Well, that's a good thing, because they're poison ivy."

Remi tried to correct me, "No, they're not . . . "

I elbowed him. "He meant they're not regular poison ivy. They're cemetery poison ivy."

I cracked my neck to the left and right, then yawned, covering my mouth with both hands.

"Marty's right." He picked up on our signal. "It's the deadliest poison ivy."

Trina shook her head. "I never heard of it."

"You didn't read about it?" Remi asked. "Marty did."

I nodded. "Cemetery ivy is a hundred times worse than regular ivy. The first thing that happens is that the person gets itchy all over."

She looked down at her hands.

Remi added, "It starts in the hand."

"Then it moves through the whole body in less than five minutes. In fact, doesn't Trina's face look red?"

I could see my friend trying to keep from grinning. "A little bit," he said.

"That's a very bad sign," I clucked.

"Why?" Trina demanded.

"It means the infection has gone to your face," I said.

She started to reach for her cheeks but stopped herself.

"I bet it feels like ants crawling up your face," he said.

"I'm not itchy," she claimed, but her nose twitched.

"Do you know what the worst thing about cemetery poison ivy is?" I asked. "It's what happens if you don't scratch."

"What happens?" Trina leaned forward.

"You'll grow a beard of leaves," I said. "Scratching stops the ivy from taking root."

Remi shuddered. "You'll have a face of dandelions. Not the pretty yellow ones, but the ugly ones with fuzzy white heads."

"Yes, and you'll have to shave every day," I added.

Trina scrubbed her face. "Ew. Gross! Get it off! Get a doctor. I'm going to have weed face!"

As she danced around the tombstones, scrubbing her cheeks, I smirked. This was great revenge for all the times she picked on me, but when she didn't stop screeching, I started to feel a weird flutter in my chest. I felt like I was listening to a baby cry; I had to make her stop.

"Relax," I said. "There's no such thing as cemetery poison ivy."

"He's lying," Remi said. He whispered to me, "Don't let the monkey butt off the hook."

She stopped scratching. "What do you mean?"

"I made up the ivy story to prove you were hiding in the bushes," I said.

"You're no fun," he said, elbowing me in the ribs.

Trina glared at us, "You won't find it so funny when I tell everyone I caught the two of you Crossing The Line."

"No one's Crossed The Line," I said. "It's just a coincidence that we're here at the same time."

"*Hel-lo.* I know you're friends. I've been following you everywhere. The library. The hardware store. And now here. I know you've been trying to catch this Graffiti Ghoul. Except, you're on the wrong track. It's not one ghoul; it's a bunch of them."

"How do you know?" I asked.

Trina took off her backpack, unzipped it and reached in. She pulled out a piece of wood, the broken piece from the shed door. One side was blank, but the other side had a spray-painted "s".

"I found this near the shed. It fits at the end of 'Ghoul'," she said, smugly trumping our investigation with her evidence. "The real message was 'Ghoul*s* Rule'."

More than one "Ghoul." Why hadn't I figured out that the "s" might have been missing from the word "Ghoul"? Did this confirm my theory that the Gangstas were responsible for the graffiti? If Trina had the "s", what other clues did we miss and she find? Was she a better detective than Remi and me?

"What else do you know?" I asked, pretending not to be interested.

"That's none of your business," Trina said.

"Why do you even care about this case? You think you're Nancy Drew?" Remi said.

She shot back, "You two think you're the Hardy Boys."

"There's nothing wrong with the Hardy Boys," I said.

"There's nothing wrong with Nancy Drew."

"She's a girl," Remi said. "Like you."

"Well, this girl is taking over the graffiti case."

"Says who?" I said.

"*Hel-lo.* I'm Litter Patrol Leader," Trina said. "Graffiti is litter, and this is my jurisdiction."

"Who's Jerry Dixon?" Remi asked. "Is he related to Franklin Dixon, the guy who wrote the Hardy Boys?"

I could figure out the meaning of hard words by listening for the smaller words that made up the big word. "Juris" reminded me of Jurassic, the dinosaur age. "Dick" was old-time slang for a private detective, and "shun" meant to stay clear of, or avoid. Putting them all together, I figured "jurisdiction" meant that Trina thought we were extinct dinosaur detectives and wanted us out of her way.

"She's telling us to drop the case," I explained.

"Forget it," he said.

I agreed with my best friend. "We found the graffiti first. We found the can of spray paint. And we're going to find the criminal. We don't need another partner."

"I'm not going to be your partner. I'm going to be your boss, and you're going to be . . . my Nancies." She grinned wickedly.

"Nancies?!" Remi blurted. "No way."

"You can't make us do anything," I said.

"Sure I can. I'm using my authority as Litter Patrol Leader to make you my Nancies. And now I'm going to delegate you your assignments."

"What's that mean?" he whispered.

"It's when I tell other people to do work and I get the credit when the job is done," said Trina.

"You can't make us work for you," I said.

"I can make your lives miserable," she threatened.

"You gonna tell everyone we Crossed The Line?" Remi asked, sneering.

"There're worse things than ninety-nine nurples." Her cold voice sent shivers up my spine. What was worse than ninety-nine nurples? She turned and started to walk away.

I whispered to Remi, "Don't get her mad."

He whispered, "She's bluffing. Besides, we'll crack this case before she can do anything to us."

I hoped my friend was right, because I was pretty sure that no amount of garlic could ever stop Trina.

THIRTEEN

The next day things were different at school. No one made fun of my fuzzy pants. No one joked that I should change the Band-Aid that held the bridge of my glasses together. No one even looked my way. While I appreciated the break from teasing, I sensed something was up. Maybe the kids were gearing up for a huge tease attack and were ignoring me so I'd let my guard down. Remi would know why everyone was treating me this way; he had the inside dirt on all schoolyard tricks, French or English.

When I reached the Jesus statue, I spotted my friend sitting alone on the stone steps leading to the second floor of our school. I couldn't help but think how weird this seemed, because normally Remi was surrounded by his French friends. Now, the same guys were veering around him like he was contagious, or worse: like he was the stinky kid. Something was definitely wrong.

A group of French girls walked past the statue, whispering and pointing at Remi. I tiptoed behind them to eavesdrop, inching along the invisible line like a tightrope walker. A girl in sweat pants and a pink top chewed on a huge wad of gum.

She nodded toward Remi. "You know what kind of people live in those places, don't you?"

The other girls leaned forward.

"Criminals," the gum girl answered.

A girl with super-thick glasses added, "I heard trailer park people are so poor they don't even have running water. Do you know what else, Natalie? I heard they steal it to take a bath."

"You think that's bad, Denise? I heard they go to the bathroom against fire hydrants like dogs," Natalie said.

"Gross," the other girls chimed.

A girl with blonde pigtails raised her hand.

Natalie nearly spit out her gum from laughing. "Colette, we're not in class. You don't have to ask permission to talk."

Colette lowered her hand. "What's so bad about living in the trailer park?"

Denise asked, "Do you like stepping in pee?"

"No one pees outside," Colette argued.

Natalie stepped forward. "How do you know?"

Colette said nothing.

Denise guessed, "I bet she lives in the trailer park too."

Colette looked down at her feet.

"She does," the girls said.

Natalie sneered. "You're T.P. trash?"

Denise nodded. "We should've known. You smell funky, like a fire hydrant."

The other girls agreed, repeating Natalie's insult. Colette backed away, accidentally bumping into me.

"Sorry," she mumbled.

"My fault," I said.

"Colette's always tripping over her big feet," said Denise, her eyes as big as dinner plates behind her thick glasses.

Natalie agreed. "Accident magnet."

Denise added, "Clown-Feet Colette."

Colette tried to hide her right foot behind her left leg but lost her balance and stumbled into me again. Everyone laughed.

"Your feet don't look big," I said.

"Thanks," Colette mumbled.

"Get away from him," Denise warned. "You'll get Chinese cooties."

Natalie laughed. "And then your eyes'll turn slanty."

I felt a case of *teasitus* coming on fast.

"Do you have cooties?" Colette asked me.

"What does it matter?" Natalie answered before I could. "She's T.P. trash anyway. She already has cooties."

"It's not called a trailer park," I said. "It's Forest Heights Estates."

"Who cares?" Denise said.

Natalie laughed. "Do you hang out with T.P. trash?"

"Who else would be friends with the *Chinois*?"

"Go back to where you came from," Natalie said. "Go back to China."

I wanted to tell Natalie that I was born in Canada and that I never saw China, but if my force field couldn't stop teasing then nothing could, especially not talking back. The only thing that worked was to walk away, which I did.

"That's not nice," Colette said. "You shouldn't pick on him."

Denise teased, "Why don't you go sit with your T.P. boyfriend over there?"

Sure enough, standing up against teasing only invited more teasing.

Natalie yelled loud enough so I could hear. "You two can get married on the Boudreau Bus."

Denise smirked. "The T.P. transporter."

"The smelly-pee shuttle," Natalie said.

"The Loser-Bago," Denise said, laughing.

Silence. Her joke failed.

"Loser-Bago. The opposite of Win-a-bago . . . " Denise started to explain.

I couldn't be bothered with the rest of her explanation, because I had to talk to Remi. He moped on the steps, looking down at the cement sidewalk.

"Smelly sneakers," I whispered, giving the code phrase for our secret meeting place when we couldn't meet at the Jesus statue.

I headed to the boot room, which was the only place where the French and English kids could be together, but no one spent much time in the room because it was full of smelly sneakers. It was the perfect secret meeting place. Remi shambled into the boot room, looking pale like he had a severe case of *teasitus*.

"Are you okay?" I asked.

"Duh! Do I look like I'm okay? Every monkey butt at school knows I live in the trailer park."

"I know. I heard the French girls talking."

"How did everyone find out?" he asked.

"There's only one person who could spread rumours this fast," I said. "Trina."

"But it's not a rumour. How did she find out?"

"Maybe she followed us after the graveyard. She did say she'd find something worse than ninety-nine nurples."

"She did. None of my friends'll talk to me now. You don't know how that feels."

"*I'm* talking to you."

"But no one else will," he said. In just a day, my friend had travelled from Cool Country to Alien Nation, once a population of me.

"We have to get Trina to take it back," I said.

In the schoolyard the gossip queen perched on the leathery seat of a swing, waiting for her subjects to kneel before her. She drank from a slushie cup and broke into a strawberry-covered smile when she saw us.

"Did you think you'd get away with it?" I asked.

"What are you talking about, Marty?" She batted her eyelashes, pretending to be innocent.

"You told everyone about Remi," I accused.

"So I told a little white lie." Trina sucked on her slushie straw, grinning. "So what?"

She had no idea her story was true!

"You did this to get us to work for you?" Remi asked.

She played with the bendy straw. "I like to get things my way."

"Do you really think we'll help you now?" I asked.

She let go of her straw. "Of course."

"Why?" he demanded.

She sighed. "If you're working for me on the graffiti case, then there's a perfectly good reason why you were near the trailer park yesterday, and you can tell everyone that."

"What's stopping us from telling everyone about the case now?" I asked.

"*Hel-lo*. They won't believe you. They'll only believe me. I'm the one who started the rumour; I'm the only one who can end it."

As much as I hated to admit she was right, Trina had a point. Gossip was like riding a bike down a steep hill. A little pedal power moved the bike down the slope, and gravity did the rest. Once the bike reached top speed, almost no one could stop it. The only person who even had a chance of slowing down the bike was the person riding it. All Trina had to do was squeeze the brakes and the gossip would roll to a stop.

"Forget it," Remi said. "I'm not working for a snot gobbler."

"I'm giving you a way out," she said. "Do you want people to believe you live in the trailer park?"

I knew he didn't want people to know the truth, but Trina had Remi so mad that he didn't see the value of her offer. Once he'd made up his mind, he never backed down. Last summer, we fired slap shots against the cement wall of my parents' store. The ball kept rolling into dips in the gravel parking lot, so he could never connect properly. Instead of moving the ball to level ground, he whacked at it from the same place a hundred times, getting madder and madder until he finally smacked the ball so hard that it sailed on to the roof and rolled into the gutter, where it stayed. I worried that this same stubborn streak would leave him stuck on a roof with no way down.

"I'm not going to be your slave," he said, turning and walking away.

"I'll give you until the end of the day to change your mind," Trina called after him, but he was too far away to hear her.

"Remi! Wait up," I called, starting after him.

"Your friend's making a big mistake," she said, stopping me.

"There's got to be something else we can do," I said.

"Nope," she said, her tongue bright pink from her slushie drink.

I watched my friend walk away, unsure of what to do to help him. Eric Johnson and Lawrence Bennet walked past me.

The rat-faced Lawrence nibbled his fingernails. "Last week I saw the T.P. kid beside my locker, and now I can't find my pencil."

"Yeah, my homework was missing yesterday," Eric said.

Lawrence laughed. "That's because you didn't do it."

"Oh yeah. You were supposed to do it for me."

Lawrence stopped laughing.

Eric smiled. "Kidding. You're supposed to do my homework *this* week."

They walked away, snickering. I'd been teased enough to know that it wouldn't be long before the teasing would go from behind Remi's back to right in his face. The only way to save my best friend was to make a deal with Trina, my worst enemy.

FOURTEEN

"**R**aise your right hand," Trina ordered.

"Why?"

"*Hel-lo*! I'm going to swear you in as a Litter Patrol deputy."

"Do I get a badge?"

"No, but I'll let you drink some of my swamp water." Trina constantly pushed her slushies on people.

"No way. You were drinking from that straw," I said.

"Whatever," Trina said. "Raise your hand."

"Wait a minute. How do I know you'll hold up your end of the deal?"

"I'll swear on it," she said.

"How do I know you won't break your word?"

Her red-stained mouth dropped open, offended. "An oath is the most important of all promises. I'd never break it. Ever."

"Unless you're lying to me now."

"Do you remember the spelling bee last year?"

How could I forget? Our grade three teacher, Ms. Connor, ran the competition in her classroom, and sent bad spellers back to their desks one after the other until only Trina and I were standing at the head of the class. We spelled thirty-five words correctly in a row, going back and forth; neither of us missed a single word. Trina acted like the words she had to spell were too easy and the words I had to spell were no-brainers, but she lost when she spelled "alienate" with two "L"s, and I spelled the word correctly. That victory put me on top of the world for a whole week.

"Sort of," I said.

"When you beat me, I swore I'd make your life miserable."

I thought she picked on me because I looked different. Maybe if I lost the next spelling bee to Trina, she'd stop.

"Do you promise to stop the gossip about Remi?" I asked.

She nodded. "As soon as I get even."

"What do you mean get even? He didn't do anything to you," I said.

"*Hel-lo.* He started that rumour about me having a stupid crush on you."

The image of Trina kissing me leapt into my mind again. Why couldn't I stop thinking about it?

"Everyone believes I'm a freak-a-zoid because they think I'm after you," she said, "and it's all Remi's fault. I have to get even."

In some ways, Remi and Trina were exactly alike. They had the same Newtonian sense of justice and identical stubborn streaks.

"When will you be *even*?" I asked.

"When he apologises."

The chances of Trina getting an apology were as good as my chances of becoming popular. I still had to do something to save Remi, but I had nothing to offer . . . except the key to solving the mystery.

"What if I brought you the spray paint instead?" I suggested. "We were planning to dust it for finger-prints in the science lab after school. If you have the can, you can find out who painted the graffiti and you'd become the hero . . . "

"Heroine," she corrected.

I nodded. "Everyone will know that you cracked the case. They'll think the reason why you follow people is because you're like a Hardy Boy."

"Nancy Drew," she corrected. "She's a better detective."

Bad idea to argue. Instead, I agreed with Trina and used her own words to win her over. I had used this tactic with grown-ups a lot; for some reason, people liked to agree with me when I repeated their words.

"Trina, you'll be the heroine of the school. Just like — no, better than Nancy Drew. No one'll ever remember you had a crush on me."

"I never *had* a crush on you," Trina said. "They were horrible lies."

"Right. They'll just remember that the head of the Litter Patrol did a great job."

She smiled.

"And then you can tell people that you were wrong about Remi."

"Fine, fine," she said. "Now raise your right hand. I'm going to swear you into the Litter Patrol."

She raised her right hand and motioned me to put up mine. She was taking her Litter Patrol duties way too seriously, but that didn't mean I had to.

"Repeat after me," she said. "I, state your name, do solemnly swear."

"I, state your name, do solemnly swear," I repeated after Trina.

"No. Say *your* name."

"No. Say *your* name," I repeated.

"Your name."

"Your name."

"Stop repeating everything I say."

"Stop repeating — "

She clamped her hand over my mouth. "Let's start over. Repeat after me starting now. I, Marty Chan, do solemnly swear."

She uncovered my mouth.

"I, Marty Chan, do solemnly swear," I said.

She continued, "To uphold the laws of the Litter Patrol."

"To uphold the laws of the Litter Patrol."

"To listen to Trina Brewster and do everything she tells me to do."

"Everything?" I asked.

"To listen to Trina Brewster and do *everything* she tells me to do without question."

I repeated, "To listen to Trina Brewster and do everything she tells me to do without question."

She lowered her hand, but I kept mine up.

"We're not done swearing yet," I said. "You have to swear to your part of the deal."

Trina fumed for a second, then raised her hand. "Okay. I swear I'll stop the rumours about Remi . . . after I have the can of spray paint."

"Now we have a deal," I said.

"I want the can by the end of the day or the deal's off."

"You'll have it."

This wasn't going to be easy. The spray paint was locked up safe and sound in Remi's locker. I'd have to come up with a pretty good excuse to take it without making him think I didn't trust him any more. I decided to tell him that, with the other kids watching for chances to razz him, the can might be safer with me.

As I walked past Remi, I pretended my shoelace had come undone. I kneeled and took my time "tying" my shoe.

"Smelly bum," I whispered, our code phrase for meeting in the boys' bathroom.

Before he could move, I spotted Jean and Jacques Boissonault walking toward us. The brothers nudged each other and snickered. I knew that cruel laugh; it was the chuckle right before a bully said something nasty to me. I straightened up and waited.

"Hey, Jean. Do you like *trash*?"

Jacques said, "I hate *trash*."

They looked at Remi, who glared back, but said nothing.

Jean Boissonault added, "Especially trailer *trash.*"

The brothers laughed and walked away, completely ignoring me. The teasing would only get worse for Remi.

"Smelly bum," I repeated.

"Keep away," he whispered. "Or they'll think I Crossed The Line too." He scooted away like I had cooties.

I caught up. "Smelly bum," I said.

Denise overhead me. "Yeah, Remi does have a smelly bum."

"I wasn't saying that he stunk," I tried to explain.

Too late. Denise shuffled down the hall, warning people to steer clear of Remi's smelly bum. He glared at me, then walked away. I should have told Denise to stop being cruel, but I didn't; I knew I'd create more trouble if I said anything, just as Colette did when she tried to stand up for me. Instead I skulked off to class.

At lunch hour the kids hounded Remi. He headed outside with a wild pack of Tease Terriers nipping at his heels. I'd never be able to get near him, and I really needed to get the can of spray paint. Desperate times called for desperate action. If I couldn't get my friend to open his locker, I'd have to do it myself.

In television shows I'd seen people pick locks by listening for clicks. I pressed my ear close to his combination lock as I turned the dial. Only the sound of my guilty heartbeats filled my ears; I hated what I was doing, but there was no other way. *Tick.* Was that the first number? The dial read 34. The back of Remi's hockey jersey was 34. Was this a coincidence? No. This had to be the first number.

I spun the dial in the opposite direction. Any minute someone could come around the corner and catch me in the act, but I had to move slowly or else I'd miss hearing the *tick.* Footsteps echoed down the hall. No time to waste; I had to move faster. My sweaty hand slipped on the combination dial, and the lock banged against the metal door. I looked around, half expecting The Rake to barrel down the hallway and send me to his office. I stepped away from the locker and leaned against the wall, forcing my shaking leg to stand still. I waited for what seemed like forever, until I was sure no one was coming.

Back to the lock. I slowly turned the dial, straining to hear the tumbler. Sweat streamed down my forehead. I wiped it away on the back of my sleeve as I listened for the . . . *tick.* The dial stopped on the number 10. What did ten mean to Remi? He was ten years old. He had ten fingers. He had ten toes. He sometimes counted to ten when he was mad. Ten had to be the second number. I wiped my sweaty palms on my pants and spun the dial in the opposite direction, my confidence growing. I put my ear to the lock, waiting for the final *tick* that would spring the lock open.

Ker-plang! Remi smacked his hand on the metal locker door. I jumped back, my ears ringing from the loud bang. I had concentrated so hard on listening to the lock that I didn't hear my friend sneak up on me.

"What are you doing?" he asked.

"It's not what it looks like."

"You want the can for yourself," he accused. "You don't want to catch Graffiti Ghoul with the T.P. punk."

"You've got it wrong."

"Then why are you trying to break into my locker?"

"I can't tell you," I said. He'd never understand the deal I made with Trina.

"Get out," he said, pushing me away from his locker. "One . . . two . . . three . . . "

"Please, Remi."

"Now." He pushed me again.

I stumbled backward, right into The Rake.

"What's the fuss about, gentlemen?" he asked.

"Nothing," Remi muttered.

To a grown-up, the word "nothing" was like a potato chip. No adult could stop with one. Now that he had a taste of it, Mr. Henday craved the entire bag. He crossed his arms and placed his finger in tapping position. "Do you two want a strike?"

Remi couldn't afford another strike on his record, and I was the one who was in the wrong.

"It's my fault," I said. "I thought this was my locker."

"And where's your locker, Mr. Chan?"

I pointed down the hall to the English side of the school.

"That's a pretty big mistake to make, don't you think?"

My titanic excuse had just hit The Rake's iceberg, and it was sinking fast. I wished I had a life preserver to keep my lie afloat, but I went under, saying nothing.

"Mr. Boudreau, why were you pushing Mr. Chan?"

Remi shrugged.

"You boys do know that fighting counts as a strike."

"I'm the one who started it," I said. "You shouldn't give him the strike. I'm the one who deserves it."

"This is a new one. Someone *wants* to get a strike. There must be something very important in that locker," Mr. Henday said.

"No," I lied.

"What's in the locker?"

"Nothing," I blurted.

I had fed our principal another potato chip.

"Mr. Boudreau, open the locker. Now."

Remi glared at me. Behind him, Trina led a group of kids through the hall. They all sipped slushies.

"Move along, people," Principal Henday ordered. "Nothing to see here."

He had just whetted their appetites with his own "nothing" potato chip. The kids walked in slow motion, almost like zombies. Trina sucked on her slushie straw and stared at the locker while Remi dialed his combination. KA-CHUNK. He unhooked the lock and stepped back. Mr. Henday opened the locker, reached in and pulled out a can of spray paint. The kids buzzed around us like flies over a garbage can full of pork fat.

"It's not mine," Remi said.

"Mr. Boudreau, don't make it any worse by lying."

"I found it," he said. "I was going to turn it in."

I backed up my friend. "Mr. Henday, I can tell you the whole story — "

Trina coughed and gave me a 'shut up' look.

"I want to hear the story from Mr. Boudreau."

Remi looked down and said nothing. Mr. Henday shook his head. "Let's go to my office and discuss this."

He put his hand on Remi's shoulder and turned him toward the office.

"Mr. Henday," I started.

Trina coughed another warning, but I ignored her. I had to help my friend.

"The spray paint isn't his. Trina knows the truth." I grabbed her arm and pulled her forward. "Tell him about the clues you found."

She squirmed out of my grasp and stepped away, glaring, but she shrivelled under The Rake's curious gaze.

"Ms. Brewster, do you know anything about this?"

"I don't know what he's talking about," she said, staring straight ahead.

Mr. Henday folded his arms and tapped his elbow. "Really?"

Tap. Tap. Tap. Trina shifted from one foot to the other, trying not to look at The Rake's finger of interrogation. Tap-tap-tap-tap. Principal Henday poured on the pressure. Tap-tap-tappity-tap-tap. Trina looked down at her pink sneakers. Why wasn't she taking credit? Maybe she needed some prompting.

"Trina found the paint," I lied. "Remi was just holding the can for her."

"I never saw that can in my life," she said, passing on her big chance to be the heroine.

"She told me she wanted to turn it in to you," I said.

"My friends and I were buying slushies at the gas station. How could I tell you to do anything?" She shrugged and held out her hands, playing dumb.

Principal Henday closed the locker. "Enough games, Mr. Chan. All of you get to class before I issue strikes."

The kids scattered like a bunch of bats.

"No running!" The Rake roared.

The kids slowed down. My enemy race-walked to class while my best friend shambled to the principal's office. It should have been the other way around. As I watched The Rake lead Remi away, a horrible thought dawned on me. Maybe Trina had never wanted credit for finding the can of spray paint. Maybe she wanted to pin the graffiti crime on someone, and I had just helped her frame my best friend. The only reason why she'd want to do that was clear: Trina Brewster was Graffiti Ghoul.

FIFTEEN

All the clues added up. The other day, when I'd called Shane "Ghoul," Trina had looked up. At first I thought my whispering was annoying her, but now I knew the truth. She had followed Remi and me to the hardware store and the graveyard; only a criminal worried about being caught would follow the detectives. Of course she'd want the can of spray paint, because she wanted to destroy the evidence. And if she couldn't destroy it, then she'd find a fall guy, which explained why she lied to The Rake about never seeing the can before.

But if Trina was the graffiti artist, why did she rip off the "s" from the original message? Was she a living member of the Gangstas? Did she know Dylan Green, the name on the tombstone surrounded by the beer bottles? Most important of all, what did "Ghouls Rule" mean to her?

I needed to learn more about ghouls, and not Monique's scary version. I needed real answers. That meant a visit to the school library. Between the stacks of non-fiction books and the four Internet stations, I was sure I'd find Trina's connection to "Ghouls Rule."

The school librarian, Ms. Tyler, waved as I entered. Unlike the town librarian, Ms. Tyler liked noise. She talked to everyone, recommending books to read, offering help with computers and telling people facts about everything in the world, from why a dog wags its tail to how fish breathe. She talked so much that students had to shush her. Ms. Tyler reminded me of a Labrador puppy: small, black-haired, full of energy, always happy to see people and constantly yipping.

"Marty, you're just in time," she called. "The books I ordered came in. You can be the first to pick. I have one that you'll love. It's a mystery."

No time for mystery stories; I was in the middle of a real-life whodunit. "Maybe later, Ms. Tyler. I have to do some work on the computer," I said.

"Do you need help?" she asked, rolling up the sleeves of her black sweater. "I've found a new search engine that I want to test out."

"Thanks, but I can do it myself."

"What are you looking up?" Ms. Tyler hopped around the library counter; if she had a tail, it'd be wagging.

"I'm looking up monsters," I said.

"Halloween's over."

"I know, but I wanted to learn more about some of the monsters I saw running around on Halloween night."

She rushed over. "I have a few books that might help. Tell me what kind of monsters."

I whispered, "The dead kind."

"Vampires? Ghosts? Frankenstein's monster? I have books on all of those." She couldn't wait to fetch them for me.

"Sure," I said, tossing her a bone. "All of them."

"I won't be long." She scampered to the stacks of books at the other end of the library.

I slid quickly in front of an Internet station. The screensaver was a fake aquarium with exotic fish. One swoosh of the mouse and the fish tank disappeared. I double-clicked on the Internet icon, called up a search engine, typed in "ghoul," and waited.

At one of the library windows, Colette, the French girl with the pigtails, looked out into the schoolyard. I remembered how the other French girls treated her when they thought she lived in Forest Heights Estates, and I wondered if their accusations were even true. That was the problem with gossip. It didn't have to be true; it just had to be said aloud.

Beep. The search engine had found my answers: 440,000 matches for "ghoul." The first page alone had four Web sites for an old movie about ghouls, three sites for video games, and two sites about a band named "The Glockenspiel Ghouls." I clicked on a link for a site that didn't have anything to do with movies, games or music. The screen went blank for a second, then a cartoon zombie in a tuxedo shambled to the middle of the screen, put on a top hat and tap danced while cheesy organ music played Happy Birthday. At the song's end, the zombie reached behind his back, pulled out a brightly-wrapped gift box and moaned "Happy Fiftieth Birthday." It was a site for people to send creepy greeting cards.

I clicked out of the screen and scanned the next listings. They offered the same kinds of sites as the first screen, some even with the same Web addresses. How was I ever going to find the truth?

Ms. Tyler bounded to me, happily carrying a large book. "Sorry I took so long. Why is that when you're looking for something, it's always in the last place you look?"

"Why would you keep looking after you found it?" I asked.

She laughed. "That's why it's always in the last place I look. Very clever."

I thought it was just common sense.

"You're in luck. This encyclopedia gives great descriptions and even some drawings of monsters. Look at this one of the Cyclops."

"Who?"

She covered one eye and tromped around the computer station, acting like One-Eyed Pete. "From the Greek story, *The Odyssey*."

"Are there ghouls in it?" I asked.

She shook her head, then noticed the computer screen. "Ooh. Ghouls. What do you want to know about them?"

"Where they come from," I said.

"Ah. I might be able to help you out there."

Ms. Tyler's knowledge of trivia might come in handy today; I might not need to sift through 440,000 web sites.

"Where do ghouls come from?"

"Don't believe what they tell you in the movies. The real story is much scarier."

She explained that the myth of ghouls, also known as zombies or the walking dead, began long ago in a village on an island called Haiti. One day, a villager died mysteriously in his sleep. His wife mourned for him and buried him in the graveyard, but when his brothers visited the cemetery the next day, the grave had been dug up and the body was missing. Some superstitious villagers believed the dead man crawled out of the ground himself and became a zombie. This sounded suspiciously similar to Monique's story about the Gangstas. I peeked around, expecting Brian to jump out and scare me.

"That's not what really happened," Ms. Tyler said. "A visitor, a man from far away, had drinks with the villager, and he slipped a secret potion into the villager's cup, which put him into a deep sleep. Nothing could wake the villager up."

"My dad sleeps like that on Sundays. Except he snores so loud that it sounds like an airplane is landing in the living room. Didn't this guy snore?"

"No. The potion paralyzed him so he couldn't move or make a sound. So when his family found him in bed, they thought he'd died. They buried him, but he was still alive. Unfortunately, the only person who knew this was the zombie-maker, who went to the graveyard at night and dug the man up."

"Why did he do that?"

"To get slaves to work on a plantation. Free labour."

"You mean like when my dad makes me take out the garbage or mop the floors?"

"Not quite."

"Wait a minute. The villager had to know he didn't belong on the plantation."

She shook her head. "The potion wiped out his memory. He couldn't remember his village or his family, and the zombie-maker convinced him that he had worked on the plantation all his life."

"Yes, but his family must have looked for him."

"They thought he was the walking dead. If they saw him, they'd run away in fear. Can you imagine your own friends and family avoiding you?"

I thought about how the French kids steered around Remi in the morning, and how everyone avoided me all the time. A person didn't need to drink a zombie potion to be treated like the undead.

"Do you know what goes in the potion?" I asked.

"The main ingredient is the poison from a puffer fish, but the rest of the recipe is a secret. No one knows for sure, and no one should ever try to make the potion. It's very dangerous. One sip and zap! You get a brain freeze, and the next thing you know you're a zombie."

Brain freeze! The connection between Trina and ghouls became crystal clear. Zombie potions gave people brain freezes; what else gave people brain freezes? Slushies! Trina had been pushing all the kids at school to drink slushies. She wasn't a ghoul; she wanted to *make* ghouls.

"Thanks, Ms. Tyler. That's all I need to know."

"Wait. Don't you want to take out the bo — "

I was out the library door before she finished her question. The sooner I confronted Trina, the sooner I'd clear Remi's name. But classes were over and most kids had gone home; the only ones left were The Rake's troublemakers, who had to serve detention. Shane Baxter lumbered out of the cafeteria, which doubled as the detention hall. Behind him, Natalie, the nasty French girl from the schoolyard, shuffled out. They walked toward me. She stuck her tongue out at me while he hip-checked me into the wall. Detention didn't make people behave better: it only made them meaner.

"Mr. Baxter, back in the room." Mr. Henday stood behind us.

"I was just fooling around with my good buddy," Shane claimed.

I said nothing.

"Back in detention, Mr. Baxter."

Shane shambled back to the detention hall.

"Mr. Henday, I know who really drew the graffiti," I said.

"I'm not interested. Go home, Mr. Chan."

He had made up his mind about my friend. The only way to convince The Rake of the truth was to get the zombie-maker herself to confess. Maybe I could trick her into admitting her guilt and record her. I'd seen the same tactic on TV police shows. If it worked on TV, it should work in real life.

The next morning I borrowed my parents' cassette tape recorder. The ancient machine was as big as a box of Cornflakes and as heavy as a bucket of kitty litter. On TV, the police attached tiny microphones to witnesses' stomachs with tabs of tape. The only thing that would hold this giant machine to my chest was duct tape. Lots of duct tape. After I'd fastened the tape recorder to myself, I looked like a grey mummy. The bulky contraption was so big that none of my own clothes could cover it. I had to borrow my dad's baggy brown sweater.

As I slipped into the itchy wool sweater, Mom yelled from the kitchen, "Take out the garbage before you go to school."

"Okay, Mom." The sweater sleeves hung off my arms like elephant trunks. They flapped against the slippery garbage bag and I couldn't get a good grip.

Mom turned around. "Aiya, why you wear your dad's sweater?"

"It's cold at school," I lied.

"I find you something to wear."

I worried she'd make me wear another one of her dresses. "It's okay, Mom." Quickly, I rolled up one sleeve, grabbed the plastic bag and ran to the back of the store.

"How about a scarf?" she called after me.

"The sweater's warm enough," I yelled back.

Outside, I hurled the green bag in the dumpster. The tape recorder shifted against my chest, giving me a nurple. Ouch! I tried to adjust the tape recorder into a less painful position. When I turned around, the pain went away, replaced with shock from what I saw. On the back wall of my parents' store, a yellow and red message screamed:

DON'T MESS WITH US GHOULS!

SIXTEEN

The graffiti message didn't look like the one on the school shed. The first message looked like balloons while this one looked like flames. Instead of black outlines, these letters were outlined with red. There were no artsy squiggles or star patterns around the words. The big, fat message stood out on the white cement wall, as if the painter wanted people to see the warning and nothing else. Still, I had no doubt that Graffiti Ghoul, a.k.a. Trina, had written this warning. With the words "us ghouls," she was telling me that her slushies had worked: she now had a zombie army.

Dad quietly surveyed the graffiti while Mom acted like the store was on fire, barking orders to no one in particular about cleaning the graffiti "right now!" She stormed into the store, muttering that she had to get her cleaning supplies. She popped back out a second later.

"What you waiting for?" she yelled at Dad. "We have to clean it."

She went back inside. A second later, she returned but had no supplies.

"Did your friends do this?" she yelled at me.

"No, Mom."

She ran inside the store.

Dad shook his head. "Who would do this?"

He didn't look at me. He wasn't expecting an answer.

"Why did they do this to our store?" he asked the air.

I wanted to tell him the message was meant for me, but I didn't know if he'd understand.

He wiped the wall with his butcher's apron. The paint was already dry. "What did I do to deserve this? Why not the bakery or the bar? Why me?"

A vein bulged on Dad's forehead. He yanked off his apron, but the strings knotted behind his neck. This only seemed to make him madder. He thrashed around, finally ripping the apron strings off.

"Why?" he yelled.

He hurled the apron against the message. Then he stared at the graffiti, panting like he'd been running a marathon.

"Are you okay, Dad?"

He ran his hand over his bald spot and calmed down. "I'm sorry. Never show people you are angry. Remember that."

"Can I do anything?" I asked.

"No. You go to school. I have to go check on something in the store."

Any time Dad was upset, he checked on the diapers or, more accurately, the bottle of rye he stashed behind the diapers.

"Your mom and I will clean this up." He went inside the store.

I took one last look at Trina's message, then I walked to the wall and picked up Dad's apron. As I lifted up the cloth, I noticed a glint. Underneath the apron was a shiny earring. I picked it up. Specks of red paint covered the silver trinket, which was in the shape of an "s". It was just like the "s" on the board that Trina had been carrying around. "S" stood for sneaky graffiti artist. "S" stood for shameful criminal mastermind. "S" stood for solid evidence against Trina. I pocketed her earring and went inside.

At the kitchen sink Mom filled a bucket with hot water, muttering to herself about how hard it was to remove paint and how she should have never let Dad talk her into moving to Bouvier. I tossed the apron on the counter beside her.

"You know who do this?" she asked, wringing a sponge tightly.

The image of Trina sprang to mind. She puckered for a kiss, and I shoved her back. My arch enemy smiled, flashing rotten green teeth. While she was pretty on the outside, she was nothing but a ghoul on the inside.

"You come home right after school and help me clean up the wall," Mom ordered.

"I will."

"And Marty . . . you not tell anyone about this."

"Why not?" I asked.

"I not want people talking about this. It just make more trouble."

"Okay."

But it was too late. News of the graffiti beat me to school. No one worried about Crossing The Line; French kids and English kids flocked together and chirped about what happened. When they spotted me, they flocked to me like magpies to road kill. I tried to shoo them away, but they pecked at me with questions.

"What did the graffiti look like?" Jean Boissonault asked.

Eric crowed, "My brother saw it on his way to school. He said it was bigger than the message on the school shed. Was it?"

"Where did they paint it?" Shane Baxter asked.

"What did it say?" Natalie demanded.

"Who did it?" Colette wondered.

"Do you have any enemies?" Samantha asked.

I wanted to say *everyone* was my enemy, but I promised Mom I'd say nothing about the graffiti. Instead I glared at Trina, who was part of the crowd. She looked away, saying nothing, letting her zombie army do her dirty work. The kids came up with answers to their own questions. None of their answers were right.

"I heard Marty had a fight with Remi," Natalie said.

"My brother said Remi tried to punch him, but Marty used his kung fu and knocked Remi on his back," said Jacques.

"They were fighting about the spray paint," said Eric.

"I bet Remi wrote the message on Marty's store," Shane suggested.

No way would I let this rumour catch fire. "Remi's not that kind of guy."

"You're standing up for him?" Natalie asked. "After what he did?"

"He didn't paint the graffiti," I said.

"Of course he did," Natalie said. "He's trailer trash."

"Does anyone have *proof* that he did it?" I demanded.

Colette raised her hand. The other kids giggled. She stammered, "Well, i-it's just that. I-I mean, h-he did have a can of paint in his locker."

"And he lives in the trailer park," Eric Johnson said.

"Forest Heights Estates," I corrected him.

"Only criminals live in trailer parks," Shane said.

"Forest Heights Estates," I repeated.

Colette said, "Not everyone in Forest Heights is bad."

"Says the girl who lives in the trailer park," said Natalie.

"Forest Heights Estates!" I shouted.

The kids quieted down.

"Remi's family is very nice," Colette argued. "His dad fixed our car. And his mom brought over rhubarb-apple pie last week."

Trina's eyes popped wide. "Remi *does* live in the trailer park?"

Samantha looked at Trina, puzzled. "You're the one who told us."

Trina looked down at her feet.

Jean said to Colette, "I bet his dad was gonna steal your guys' car."

Eric added, "And they stole the rhubarb apples."

"There's no such thing as rhubarb apples. It's rhubarbs and apples," said Samantha, shaking her curly brown hair.

"You mean he stole two things?" he asked.

The talk turned to how a thief got his start. Everyone became an expert. Some claimed thieves were born to steal. Others said crime had to be learned and, just like riding a bike, thieves never forgot how to steal. But everyone agreed that robbers got their start in trailer parks.

"You've got it all wrong," I said.

The kids ignored me as I tried to shout down their false rumours, all of which I was sure Trina had started. She controlled the kids with her zombie potion; they believed her every word, even when each word was an outrageous lie. I had to get her alone, away from her army of ghouls, so I could expose the truth.

"If there's graffiti in town, there might be more on the school," I said.

"I didn't see anything," Natalie said.

"Maybe it's being painted right now," I suggested.

"Where's Remi?" Jacques yelled.

The kids looked around.

Eric yelled, "Let's get him!"

Everyone fanned out across the school grounds to look for Remi, while Trina broke away from the crowd and walked to the swings. She didn't have to do anything now that she had the students under her control. Not for long, I hoped. While her back was to me, I reached under my big sweater and pushed the "Record" button on the tape machine. Music blared out of my stomach and a man with a high voice screeched out a Chinese opera song.

"Haaaaaayyyyy soooonnnn siiiiiiii jiiiiiiiiiiii!"

Wrong button. I stabbed at my stomach until I hit the stop button and the noise cut off. Lifting my sweater, I found the "Record" button, pressed it, turned and headed toward my target.

"Trina, I want to talk about the graffiti."

"Go away. I don't feel like talking to anyone," she said.

"Why did you lie to Principal Henday?" I demanded.

"I didn't lie."

"Yes you did," I accused.

"It's your word against mine," she snapped.

If my trick worked, it would be her recorded word against her spoken word, and there was no way she could argue against herself. "Admit it. You were lying."

"Bug off."

She was tougher to peel than a hard-boiled egg. "I know about the slushies," I said.

Her face turned egg white. "You d-do not," she said.

I tapped away at her tough shell. "Sure I do. You're making all the kids try them. You're getting them to go buy them at the gas station. I know the whole story."

She jumped off the swing and walked away. "No one will believe you."

I cut off her escape. She zigged; I zagged. She bobbed; I weaved. She weebled; I wobbled. I didn't fall down, but Trina's tough attitude did.

"You know what you're doing is wrong," I said.

She said nothing.

"Why are you doing it? What do you get out of the slushie deal?"

I crossed my arms and tapped my elbow while I stared into her blue eyes. Tap. Tap. Tap. She tried to act cool, but her watery eyes gave her away. Tap. Tap.

Tap. Her lips quivered. The thought of kissing them popped back in my mind. I shuddered.

"Principal Henday might go easy on you if you come clean now," I said. Tap. Tap. Tap.

The finger of interrogation worked. She finally cracked. "My uncle owns the gas station. When I get people to buy slushies, he gives me free ones. Get it?"

What did her uncle have to do with zombies? Maybe the zit-faced gas jockeys were his slushie slaves, and Trina was recruiting new ones. Unsure of the connection, I nodded and pretended her confession was old news. "So what?"

"Once you taste a slushie, you get hungry for a chocolate bar. And once you eat a chocolate bar, you get thirsty for a slushie. It goes on and on and on and on. Uncle Jerry calls it his 'circle of life.' You eat, you drink, you eat. He makes money."

How could Trina and her uncle be so cold? The very idea that they used slushies to create zombies for profit made me sick. It reminded me of TV beer commercials, where the grown-ups had perfect teeth, perfect hair and perfect eyes, and they seemed to be having great fun at a party that never ended, making TV watchers think beer drinkers were cool. The ads didn't fool me; I knew the truth. People who drank alcohol didn't look like the actors in the beer commercials; they were pot-bellied and bald like my dad, and he definitely didn't look like he was having fun. When he drank he wasn't cool; he was cranky. The ads were misleading and wrong, and so was the Brewster family slushie scam.

"You're not pushing slushies on anyone any more," I said.

"I'm getting sick of slushies anyway," Trina said.

She gave in almost too easily. I didn't buy her story. One time my mom begged Dad to stop drinking, and he promised he'd give it up. Instead, he hid his booze from Mom. I suspected Trina would go underground with her slushies, slipping the icy drinks into juice boxes and handing them out at recess to unsuspecting victims.

"That's not good enough," I said. "You have to tell Principal Henday the truth. That you're Graffiti Ghoul."

"Excu-u-s-e me?" she said. "What makes you think I'm responsible for the graffiti?"

"You lied to Principal Henday yesterday," I said. "You wanted Remi to take the blame for the graffiti, because then you could get away with your crime. Admit it, Trina Brewster. You lied."

I puffed my tape recording belly toward her to capture the confession.

"Alright, I admit it," Trina said. "The Rake looked mad, and I didn't want to get in trouble."

"Gotcha!" I lifted my dad's sweater and flashed her.

Her mouth dropped open. "Is that a tape recorder?"

"Yup. And I have your confession on tape, Trina Brewster," I spoke toward the tape recorder's built-in microphone, "or should I call you the leader of the Graffiti Ghouls?"

"I'm the Litter Patrol leader, for Pete's sake. I'm trying to catch the Ghouls, not lead them. I'm the one who found the 's' by the shed."

"Pretending to be a detective is a great cover for a criminal. No one would ever suspect you," I said. "But now I have your confession on tape."

"I might have lied to The Rake, but that doesn't mean I painted the graffiti."

"I have more proof," I said, jamming my hand into my pocket. "Does this look familiar?" I produced the earring I'd found at the store and shoved it toward her face.

Trina squinted. "What is it?"

"Your earring. It fell off when you were drawing the graffiti at my parents' store."

She pulled her blonde hair back, revealing both her ears. "*Hel-lo*, my ears aren't pierced."

She leaned forward. Her earlobes had no holes.

"But if this isn't your earring, then that means you didn't paint the . . . " The words died in my throat.

Because I found the earring by the second graffitied message, I assumed it belonged to the vandal. Because Trina encouraged kids to buy slushies, I assumed she was making zombies. Because Trina lied to Principal Henday, I assumed she had to be Graffiti Ghoul. But Trina didn't have pierced ears. She might have been pushing slushies on everyone, but the kids didn't act like zombies. Even though she lied to The Rake, it didn't mean she was guilty of the graffiti crime. Just as everyone had assumed that Remi drew the graffiti because he lived in a trailer park, I had assumed the wrong thing about Trina. Was she telling the truth now?

She snatched the earring out of my hand. "Besides, even if my mom did let me wear earrings, I'd never pick something this ugly. Only a freak-a-zoid would be into snake earrings."

I took back the earring. It wasn't in the shape of an "s". It was in the shape of a snake. Snakes. Who was into — ? The truth curled around my chest and squeezed until I blurted, "I know who the Graffiti Ghouls are!"

SEVENTEEN

"Who?" Trina asked. "Who painted the graffiti?"

"I have to go." I started to walk away, but she grabbed my arm.

"You're not going to give the tape to Principal Henday, are you?"

"Maybe," I said, still mad at what she did to Remi.

Before I could take another step, Trina tackled me. "Give me the tape."

"Let go," I screamed, clutching the tape recorder against my body.

She clawed at the duct tape, grasped a loose end and pulled. Pain raked across my skin. I ran away, but Trina had a good grip of the tape, and every time I moved, the duct tape peeled off like a caked-on Band-Aid. I couldn't go far without causing myself more pain, but I couldn't let Trina get the machine. The only way to take off a Band-Aid was to rip it off in one swift move, so maybe the only way to get out of my duct tape dilemma was to get it over with in one shot. Holding my breath, I started to run and spin at the same time. A human top, I unravelled myself. It felt like strips of my skin were flying off like potato peelings, but I held on to the tape recorder and continued to spin. Trina reeled in the duct tape like she was in a tug-of-war.

As the last strip of sticky tape ripped off my raw skin, I screamed, "O-o-o-o-o-o-o-w-w-w-w-w-e-e-e-e-!"

I staggered back, dizzy and out of control. The ground rolled back and forth like the deck of a ship on a choppy ocean. I crashed into someone and the tape recorder flew out of my hands. I tried to catch it, but I missed and landed flat on my face.

"You having fun?" a familiar voice asked.

I looked up and saw my friend holding the tape recorder. The world stopped spinning.

"Remi," I said. "I know who painted the graffiti. It's — "

He cut me off. "So you didn't want to be caught hanging out with the trailer trash. I guess you found someone else to hang out with," he accused.

"I was trying to clear your name."

"Duh! Do you think I'm stupid? You tried to break into my locker."

"She made me do it," I said, pointing at Trina.

He said in a snarky voice, "I thought you were better than the other monkey butts, but I guess I was wrong."

"Let me explain," I pleaded.

"Leave me alone." Remi shoved the tape recorder back at me and walked away.

I'd hurt my friend, my only friend, by siding with the enemy, and as much as I wanted to say it was for the right reasons, I knew that I had done the wrong thing. I never should have promised Trina the can of spray paint. I never should have tried to break into Remi's locker. I never should have betrayed my best friend.

Soft hands grabbed the tape recorder. Trina had skulked up behind me and was now trying to tear the machine away from me.

"Back off," I said, regaining my hold on the tape recorder.

"You can't turn it in. My mom will kill me."

"You should have thought of that before you lied to Principal Henday."

"I'll do anything for the tape," she pleaded.

"I don't need anything from you."

"Even Nancy Drew needed someone. You can be my Ned Nickerson."

"Who?"

"Nancy's boyfriend."

The image of Trina's puckering lips flashed before me again. "No way!"

"He also helps her solve mysteries. You can't solve the case by yourself. You need my help to clear your friend's name."

As much as I hated to admit it, she was right. Without Remi, I'd never be able to catch the real Graffiti Ghouls. He was my partner. He was the brawn to my brains. He was the guy who stood up for me. He was my only friend. But, like a Band-Aid, our friendship had been ripped off in one swift move, except the pain didn't go away. It got worse.

"Go away," I said.

"We need each other," she said.

If Trina hadn't found us at the cemetery, if she hadn't sworn me in as her deputy, if she hadn't been such a snot gobbler, I'd still have my friend. I wouldn't be alone again. It was all her fault. Still, she was the only person who could help me. The graffiti message on my parents' store was a warning that the real Graffiti Ghouls were on to me. I needed a decoy to expose them. Trina could be this decoy, but how could I trust her?

"If we're going to work together, we have to shake on it," I said. I spit into my hand and offered it to her.

She stepped back, sticking her hands under her armpits. "Ew, I'm not touching your hand."

"A spit-handshake means you're absolutely serious about being my partner. It means you'd rather break your hand than break our deal. If you want to help, this is the only way."

She eyed the tape player, and reluctantly spit into her own hand. We shook, sealing our pact.

"Ew," she squealed. "It's so gross. I can feel our spit mixing."

Her hand was soft. I felt weird about holding it, about her standing so close to me, about the tingling that spread up my arm toward my fast-beating heart. I almost forgot the reasons why I hated her. I took a long time before I finally let go of her hand.

"Done. You're going to help me get the Graffiti Ghouls to confess."

Trina wiped her hand on her sweat pants. "Where are they?"

"The high school," I answered.

At the end of the day, Trina and I headed to Vanier School. We waited until the kids cleared out of the schoolyard so no one would see us together. To be safe I walked five steps ahead of her, so if anyone saw us I could tell them she was following me. The Vanier parking lot had no cars, but I was sure the criminals would turn up here sooner or later. Beside me, Trina barely breathed as she stared through the fence's diamond pattern.

"Here's the plan," I said. "The Graffiti Ghouls don't know you, so they might slip up and brag about what they did. When they do, you'll have their confession on tape."

"How am I going to get them to talk?"

"Say you want to join them."

She gulped and looked at the empty parking lot. Forbidden territory. Then she looked back at me, chewing her lower lip, wanting to say something. She didn't.

"Are you nervous?" I asked.

"Totally." Her answer surprised me. Remi never admitted he was scared, not even when I was sure he was petrified. And I knew better than to tell him when I was scared because as soon as I did, he made fun of me. I always thought that admitting you were scared was something you were never supposed to do, but when Trina told me she was nervous, I didn't feel so bad. Maybe it was okay to admit how I really felt.

"I'm scared too," I said.

"That's good to know." Trina smiled at me. I smiled back, relieved.

"The Graffiti Ghouls are going to show up here sooner or later," I said. "Keep a lookout for their car."

"What's it look like?"

"It's blue."

"Two doors? Rust on the hood? Broken headlight? Four teenagers inside?"

"Yes. How did you know?"

"Because they're coming this way." Trina pointed down the street. "I think they're following us."

Patrick's car drove toward us. I slipped the tape recorder behind my back just as the car stopped beside us. Dough Boy leaned out the passenger window and patted the top of the car. Warren sat in the back seat beside Beth. Her black hair covered her ears, so I couldn't see if her earring was missing. Was she Graffiti Ghoul, or was this going to be another dead end? Only one way to find out.

I walked closer to the car. Patrick climbed out of the driver's seat and folded his arms on top of the car. He wasn't wearing his tongue stud today. Maybe he was tired of people not understanding him.

"Dough Boy," he said. "That the punk we caught the other day?"

"Can't be. We warned Chinatown to stay away. He wouldn't come back."

"I think Chinatown needs another warning," Patrick said.

I tried to get a closer look at Beth's ears. "I'm not on the school grounds."

"You were thinking about it," Dough Boy accused, blocking my view of the back seat.

"I wasn't," I said.

"Then what're you doing here?" Patrick demanded.

Trina came to the rescue. "He's walking me home."

The two boys chuckled.

"This your girlfriend, Chinatown?" Dough Boy teased.

My face turned beet red. "No."

"Kissy, kissy," Warren taunted from inside the car.

"He's a player," Dough Boy said.

Beth leaned out the window. "Hey, I heard what happened at your old man's store."

"Yeah, Chinatown. Terrible thing. Did your old man call the police?" Dough Boy asked.

"Yes," I said.

"They have any leads?" Beth asked.

"I'm not allowed to say." I lied, noticing Beth's snake bracelet. I needed to look at her ears. "There's a bug by your face."

She swatted at the air.

"By your ear," Trina said, picking up on my plan.

Beth fluffed her hair back, revealing her ears. A snake earring was attached to one earlobe. The other ear had nothing.

"What do you know about the investigation?" Beth asked.

"The police are close to finding out who did it," I said.

Trina nodded. "So the criminals had better be careful."

"What do you know, kid?" Dough Boy asked.

"I know that the police found some important evidence at the crime scene."

Beth and Warren straightened up in the back seat and leaned forward, staring at Trina like the Big Bad Wolf about to pounce on Little Red Riding Hood. Patrick and Dough Boy glanced at each other, nervous.

"It's police business," Trina said. "We can't tell anyone."

Beth said, "We promise we won't say anything."

"I can't talk," I said.

Dough Boy opened the car door — was he going to get out? Patrick started to walk around the front of the car.

"Marty's supposed to meet the police after he drops me off," Trina said. "They're expecting him pretty soon."

"I can give you a lift," Patrick said. "Then we can chat."

I shook my head. "Trina's mom is going to drive me."

"She's expecting us right now," Trina added.

Patrick climbed behind the steering wheel while Dough Boy grunted and slammed his door shut.

Beth glared at me from the back seat. "Be careful what you say, Chinatown. You might get on the bad side of the wrong people."

Patrick drove away slowly while everyone else in the car watched us.

Once they were gone, I turned to Trina. "Did you see the earring? There was only one."

"She's the culprit, alright."

"They're all in on it," I said.

"They were pretty nosy about the police investigation, weren't they? That's a sign that they're guilty."

"Why did you lie? The police didn't find any evidence."

"*Hel-lo*, they found the graffiti."

"But you made them think the cops found something more."

"Did I?" She batted her eyes.

"I guess you didn't say anything specific."

"It's not my fault if they jumped to conclusions."

I never knew exactly how Trina started gossip. I'd only heard the rumours after they'd been passed around and exaggerated by other kids. Now I understood her trick. She planted a seed of information and let it grow in other people's imaginations. The less she said, the bigger the rumour became. The hint that the police had serious evidence had probably grown to the size of the moon in Beth's mind.

"Right now they're probably freaking out over what the police might have," Trina said.

"They'll think the cops have the earring."

"Exactly."

"You're pretty smart for a girl," I said.

"*Hel-lo*, I'm pretty smart, period."

"Let's follow them," I said.

"They're in a car."

I pointed through the fence at Patrick's car, which had just pulled into a space in the school parking lot.

"Oh," Trina said. "Never mind."

"After you."

Trina scaled the fence fast. I'd never seen anyone move that quickly. I was impressed. We snuck through the high school grounds and crept alongside the building. Ahead of us, the gang hustled across the track field.

"They're going to the cemetery," I said. "Hurry up."

"They'll see us. It's wide open ground."

"Stick with me."

I backtracked and sprinted around the other side of the school. When I reached the fence that ran beside the highway, I ran along it. Trina followed me. When we reached the corner of the graveyard, we hopped over the fence and waded through the bushes. No sign of the gang. Staying low, we moved from tombstone to tombstone, jumping over the small markers and hiding behind the tall ones. We moved deeper into the cemetery, and hopefully closer to the Graffiti Ghouls.

As we neared an open grave, we heard voices and stopped. Trina joined me as I sat down with my back against a large tombstone. Around it were a few beer bottles. It was the tombstone Remi and I had found earlier. Trying to make as little noise as possible, I gently pressed the "Record" button on my tape recorder, but the cassette tape barely spun. The batteries were weak. I turned off the tape recorder.

"What do we do now?" I whispered. "The batteries are almost dead. I might record five seconds, but that's not enough."

Trina shushed me. "Listen."

I pushed the tape recorder to one side.

"I'm telling you Patrick, I didn't drop anything," Beth protested.

Dough Boy said, "It was probably one of your dog leashes."

"Maybe it was one of your chocolate bar wrappers," Beth shot back.

"Hey, a chocolate bar wrapper isn't evidence. It's garbage."

Warren's whiny voice interrupted, "Unless they check the DNA."

"Or they could just follow the stench to Dough Boy," Beth said.

"Stick it, Beth."

"Bite me, Dough Boy."

"Ghouls! Chill." Patrick ordered.

Dough Boy complained, "Do you have to call us Ghouls? Who came up with the lame gang name anyway?"

Beth piped up, "I like being the Ghouls."

Warren said, "Actually, it sounds kinda dumb."

"It was the name of Dylan's gang," Beth said. "If it was good enough for my brother, it's good enough for me."

Dylan. Dylan Green. The name on the tombstone we were leaning against. I re-read the inscription: "Dylan Green. Loving son and brother. Survived by parents Hank and Anne and sister Elizabeth." Beth. These Ghouls weren't the undead; they were copycats.

Dough Boy yelled, "It doesn't matter if we're the Ghouls or the Goons or the Goofs. If the cops figure out it was us, we're gonna be the Jailbirds."

"We'll be okay, Dough Boy," Patrick said. "We'll say we were taking a short cut behind the store and the graffiti was already there."

Dough Boy argued, "They'll grill us until Warren falls apart."

"None of this would have happened if Beth didn't dare Patrick to paint the graffiti on the shed," Warren said.

Beth snapped, "Don't be such a wuss."

Warren said, "We should ditch the paint before the cops bust us."

"They won't find the paint," Beth argued.

As the Ghouls argued about the paint, I smiled. Things were working out better than I had planned. All I had to do was follow them to their paint stash, and I'd break the case wide open. If I could catch the Ghouls with the spray paint, then I'd have the proof to clear Remi's name and we could be friends again.

"Marty," Trina whispered.

"Shhh," I said.

"Marty," she repeated.

"What?" I turned to Trina.

A daddy-long-legs was crawling across her nose.

"Don't say anything," I said.

"Get it off me," she hissed.

"Don't freak out." I reached over to brush the spider off Trina's freckled nose. But as my hand moved closer, the spider sensed me and skittered to her cheek. Trina started to scream. I clamped my hand over her mouth.

"Mmmmmmmmmm!" Trina was terrified.

"Quiet! I heard something," Warren said.

Silence. I flicked the daddy-long-legs off Trina's face.

"You're getting paranoid, Warren," Beth said.

"Was it the Gangsta zombies?" Dough Boy asked, teasing.

"Shut up, Dough Boy," Warren snapped.

"Oooooohhmmmm, I'm going to eat your ears, Warren."

Everyone but Warren laughed.

"It's not funny," he said.

"Okay, no more games." Patrick cut off the laughter. "Let's ditch the spray paint."

As long as they didn't notice us, we could follow them to the stash and catch them red-handed, disposing of the spray paint.

"Achooo!" Trina sneezed into my hand. I yanked it away and wiped the snot on my pants.

"Who's there?" Beth yelled.

"Like they're gonna answer," Dough Boy said, a sneer in his voice.

"Check it out," Patrick ordered.

"What if it's zombies?" Warren asked.

"There's no such thing," Beth said. "Don't be such a chicken. Go see who's there."

Crunch. Crunch. Crunch! CRUNCH! They were coming right at us.

I yelled at Trina, "Run!"

"Over there!" Warren yelled.

"Where? I don't see anyone," Beth said.

"I see someone," Patrick yelled. "Over there!"

Trina and I bolted, leaving the tape recorder behind. Tombstones whipped past us. I didn't know where I was going and I didn't care, as long as it was away from the Ghouls. We scrambled over tombstones. I jumped over a low grave marker. Trina ran around it and passed me.

"Keep running, slowpoke," she panted. I picked up the pace and caught up.

Behind us, confused shouts filled the cemetery.

"Did you see them?" Beth yelled.

"Over here I think," Warren squawked.

"No! This way," Patrick screamed.

Dough Boy called out: "No! They're over here!"

Just ahead, sunlight broke through the trees and Trina and I bolted toward the light. We pushed through the prickly bushes, hopped over the fence and burst into a stubbly field between the cemetery and Forest Heights Estates. Daylight never felt so good.

"They're coming," Trina hissed. "We have to hide."

The flat field offered no hiding spot and the schoolyard was way too open. The only place I could think of was Remi's house.

"Come on." I grabbed Trina's hand and led her across the gravel road.

Which one was Remi's? I remembered his trailer had a windmill mail box, but there were four trailers in a row that had the same mail box. I picked a white trailer, ran up the steps and banged on the door. I hoped this trailer was the right one.

"Remi! Open up," I called.

"Quiet," Trina warned.

The Ghouls' voices drifted closer but I couldn't make out what they were saying. I rapped on the door again, but no one answered. The voices came closer. We were doomed.

EIGHTEEN

Dough Boy sniffed like a hunting dog around the alley. First he checked out the trailer across the gravel lane, peeking over the fence and looking under the trailer's wooden porch. He'd spot us soon enough.

I whispered, "We've got to get off this porch."

"Follow me," Trina said. "I'm good at hiding, remember?"

Down the steps Trina crept, with me close behind. The creak of the wood sounded like fingernails across a chalkboard. Trina held up her hand, stopping me. Dough Boy didn't turn around. I started to breathe again. Trina motioned me off the creaky steps and toward a fence that divided this trailer from the one behind it.

She crawled over the fence like a Ninja. I headed to the wooden fence and started to climb, but I got stuck on the top. Trina grabbed my arm and yanked me over. I yelped, but she clamped her hand over my mouth and signalled me to crouch low. She pointed at the road that ran past the new trailer. Patrick jogged along the lane, searching for us. I didn't breathe until he ran past us. Trina and I were trapped between trailers.

"Grrrrrrrrrrrrr." Why was Trina growling?

"Shhh," I hissed.

"It's not me," Trina said. "It's him." She pointed behind her.

A giant St. Bernard drooled at us. He placed his giant paws on either side of a giant bone and let out a deep "WOOOOOF!"

I nearly crapped my pants.

"Run," I said.

Trina grabbed my shirt. "He'll chase anything that runs."

"If we stay, he's going to eat us."

"I have a dog. She doesn't like sudden movements. Back up slowly. Don't look at the bone. He thinks we're trying to take it."

We inched back from the dark-eyed beast. He stopped growling, but kept looking at us. We reached the fence and caught our breath. Suddenly a pair of pudgy hands grabbed me. Dough Boy! He pulled me over the fence. Beside him, Patrick hauled Trina up.

"Well, well, well. Look at what we have here," Dough Boy said.

"Put us down," I demanded.

"Looks like we found our spies," Patrick said.

"*Hel-lo.* We were playing with the dog," Trina said.

"You want to go back in there?" Dough Boy said.

The St. Bernard barked.

"No. No. That's okay," I said. "We're done playing."

"Hey Patrick, do you want to hang them over the fence by their ankles?" Dough Boy asked.

Patrick laughed. "Not a bad idea."

"You're going to be very sorry if you don't let us go," Trina warned.

"Shut up," Dough Boy said.

Patrick said, "You're the ones who're gonna be sorry."

"The police are expecting me," I said.

"They'll have to wait 'til you get your story straight." Then Patrick called to Warren at the end of the alley. "Hey! Get Beth. Now!"

The gawky goon waved back.

Dough Boy shook me. "What did you hear in the cemetery?"

"We heard enough," I said.

"We know you painted the graffiti," Trina said triumphantly.

Patrick chuckled. "Who's going to believe a couple of kids?"

Dough Boy agreed. "It's your word against ours."

"We have proof," I said.

"Where?" Patrick asked.

"The police have it," Trina said.

Beth and Warren arrived. Four against two — the odds didn't look good. I tried to squirm free, but Dough Boy had a good grip on me.

Warren glanced around, "Guys, we'd better move somewhere quiet before the neighbours see us and ask questions."

"We'll say we saved the kids from the dog. Isn't that right, Chinatown?" Dough Boy shook me.

Patrick snarled, "What's the evidence the cops have?"

Trina said, "Ask them."

"Chinatown, you'll tell me, won't you?" Patrick asked.

Beads of sweat poured down my forehead. "What Trina said."

"The kid looks nervous, doesn't he?" Patrick asked.

Dough Boy shook me again. "You sure the cops have this *evidence*, whatever it is?" he asked.

"Yes," I lied.

"You sure you don't have this *evidence?*"

"No. Yes." I clamped my hand over my mouth.

"Warren, search him," Patrick barked.

Warren checked my pockets while Dough Boy held me.

"Stay out of there!" I yelled. "That tickles."

Warren pulled out a used tissue, a nickel, and Beth's earring.

"This look familiar?" Warren asked Beth.

Dough Boy glared at Beth. "I knew it had to be your fault."

She ignored him. "Without evidence, Chinatown and his girlfriend can talk but no one'll believe them."

Warren looked worried. "They'll still talk."

"If you two yap about this," Patrick threatened us, "we'll come looking for you. You understand?"

I said nothing. Trina looked down.

Patrick continued, "You've got no proof against us."

"Think again!" said a familiar voice behind us.

Could it be? I hoped it was him, but I had to be sure. I looked around. Remi stood in the dog's yard petting the St. Bernard, which chewed on the giant rawhide bone and wagged its tail.

"Remi, was that your trailer?" Trina asked, pointing at the white trailer.

He nodded.

"Didn't you hear us knocking?" I asked.

"I was mad at you."

"If you *girls* are done talking, we've got some business to take care of," Dough Boy said.

"Put my friend down," Remi ordered.

"What're you going to do?" Dough Boy laughed.

"He'll call the police," I said.

Patrick looked up at Remi. "You gonna do what they tell you?"

Remi smiled. "Duh! What do you think?"

Patrick shook his head. "We'll drop your friends in an open grave and let them spend the night in the cemetery with the creepy crawlies."

Remi's smile faded.

Dough Boy ordered, "Come out of the yard. Now!" He shook me around to make his point.

"I'll come out," Remi said.

"Don't," I said, but before I could say more, Dough Boy boxed my ear. "Ow!"

Beth growled at Remi. "What's it going to be?"

He headed to the gate and unlatched it. Beth and Warren walked toward him.

When they were almost at the gate, Remi kicked it wide open and yelled, "Sic 'em, Precious!"

A monster "WOOOOFFF!" erupted from the volcano mouth of the giant dog named Precious. She barrelled out of the yard after Warren and Beth, who ran for their lives. Dough Boy dropped me and ran after them. Patrick froze as Precious ran up to him, planted her giant paws on his chest, and lunged for his face. She licked him, slobbering drool all over his mouth and nose.

"Stupid mutt." He pushed her off and wiped his face on the back of his sleeve. "Guys! Get back here."

Down the lane, the other teenagers slowed down and turned around.

I yelled to Remi, "Patrick's got the earring! Get him!"

Patrick stepped back, wrapping his arm around Trina's neck. "You think *you* can do anything to me?"

Trina bit Patrick's arm. He yelped, let go of Trina and dropped the earring.

"You little brat!" he yelled.

Trina ran into the dog yard with Precious while Remi dove to the gravel road and grabbed the earring. Patrick jumped on top of Remi and pinned him down. Beth, Warren and Dough Boy broke into a sprint toward us.

"Marty! Catch!" Remi tossed me the earring.

I caught it.

"Run!" Trina yelled.

Patrick climbed off Remi and charged after me. I took off toward the cemetery. The uneven ground was tough to run across, but I couldn't slow down. I tripped on a rut and nearly fell over, but I stumbled forward until I regained enough momentum to stay upright.

Behind me, Patrick tripped on the same rut and went down. "You can't run from me forever!" He yelled.

I climbed over the cemetery fence and looked back. Beth was helping Patrick up. There was no sign of Remi or Trina. Did they get away? I hoped so.

I ran through the prickly bushes and sprinted into the graveyard, zipping past the stone markers. The only sound I could hear was my own breathing. Patrick was right. I couldn't run forever, but I couldn't stop either. As I leapt over a low tombstone, my foot caught the edge. I sprawled on the ground and skidded to a halt in front of a headstone. Behind some weeds, there were four cans of spray paint. Jackpot! I scooped up the cans, which rattled against each other in my arms. I froze, hoping Patrick and Beth didn't hear me. I listened for footsteps. Nothing.

Whew. I loaded the cans into my giant corduroy pants. Now I was glad Mom had bought me such big pants — all four cans fit snugly inside the waistband. I hoped Trina and Remi got away from the teenagers and called the police. I hoped I could get out of the cemetery before the Ghouls caught me.

The last of the sunlight faded, leaving the cemetery in eerie darkness. I started toward the fence that separated the graveyard from the high school track field. The cans clicked against each other as I moved. When I stopped, the clicking also stopped, but now I could hear the Graffiti Ghouls crashing through the cemetery as they looked for me. It sounded like they were all around. I had to find a hiding spot, but where could I go?

I walked around the corner and tripped over my tape recorder. I picked it up, wondering if there was enough power to record a cry for help. Then my foot slipped on some loose dirt and I almost fell into the open grave. I started to back away, but then a thought stopped me. Patrick had threatened to throw me in the hole, which meant it would be the last place he'd look for me. But there was a good reason why; only dead people went inside graves. I shuddered at the thought of jumping in.

"I think he's over here!" Beth yelled, sounding very close.

I had no choice. No time to waste, I tucked the tape recorder under my arm and climbed into the open grave. Please be empty, I thought. The last thing I needed to deal with was a real ghoul. I landed on soft dirt in complete darkness. I tapped my foot around the hole, feeling for a zombie that might've been down here with me. I was alone. At least I was safe from the undead; too bad my problem was with the living.

"Patrick, you see the little brat?" Beth asked, her voice sounding like it was directly over me.

"No," Patrick said, panting. "That kid's fast."

Beth sounded angry. "He's got to be here somewhere."

"We should get out of here. If the other kids got away from Dough Boy and Warren, the cops'll be here any minute."

"We're not leaving until we get my earring," Beth said.

"At least let's get rid of the paint," Patrick said.

"Good idea."

Footsteps ran away from me.

"They're gone!" Patrick yelled from further away. "The punk took them."

"Slanty Eyes couldn't have gone far."

I shifted toward the far end of the grave and crouched low. The cans clicked against each other. I froze.

"Did you hear that?"

"He's in the hole!" Patrick shouted.

Beth yelled, "Get him!"

"Oooooommmmmmm." I moaned, pretending to be a zombie. "I smell feet go-oo-ood enough to-ooo-oo eeeeeeaaattt."

"Nice try, Chinatown," Beth said. "We know it's you. Pull him out, Patrick."

Arms reached into the hole. I ducked low, avoiding them for the moment. The tape recorder dug into my armpit. Stupid thing. If the batteries had been working I wouldn't be in the hole right now; I'd be at the police station playing the Ghouls' confession. A hand grabbed my jacket. Another hand caught my hair. I yelped as they began to lift me out of the hole. Last chance. I cranked up the volume on the tape recorder, punched the "Play" button, and dropped the machine.

Patrick and Beth hauled me out. I tried to scramble away, a couple of cans slipping out of my pants. He grabbed my leg while she tried to pry my hands open.

"We have to get out of here," I said. "The Gangstas are going to climb out of the grave and eat us."

Patrick punched the back of my thigh. "Shut up and give us the earring."

Beth had almost pried open my right hand. "Give it up."

"Wait a minute," Patrick said. "Do you hear that?"

From the grave, a Chinese man's voice moaned: "Haaaaaayyyy soooonnnnnn saaaiiiiiiiii jiiiiiiiiiiiii."

"Was anyone else in the hole with him?" Beth asked Patrick.

He shook his head. "This is too creepy."

"Moooohhh fuuuuunnnnnnn gggguuuuuumm." The Chinese opera singer at ultra-slow speed sounded positively undead.

Patrick and Beth backed away from the open grave.

"It's a zombie," I said. "I'm getting out of here."

I struggled to get up, but Patrick pushed me down and vaulted over me. "Every man for himself!"

"Looooiiiiiiiiiii . . . " The weak batteries finally gave out and the creepy Chinese opera singer faded out.

Beth grabbed my arm. "Nice trick. *Not*. Now give me the earring or I toss you in the hole with whoever's down there."

I held up the earring. "You want it? Go get it."

I tossed the earring into the grave.

She grabbed my wrist and squeezed hard. "You're going in."

She pulled me toward the open grave. I dug my heels into the soft dirt, resisting. One foot slipped into the hole. I stepped back on solid ground, trying to pull away from Beth but she had a firm grip. I stomped on her booted foot, but it must have had steel toes because she didn't yelp. Desperate, I dipped low and licked her hand, mimicking Precious' wet slobbers.

"Gross!" she yelped, letting go.

I jumped back from the open grave and tried to run away, but Beth snagged the back of my collar. She dragged me toward the open hole. This time I was sure I was going in. Suddenly, flashing red and blue lights lit up Beth's face and her furrowed eyebrows. A police cruiser, its lights flashing, rolled into the cemetery and cut off Patrick's exit. He slowly raised his hands. Busted. In the back seat I could see someone fat and short and someone tall and skinny; they had to be Dough Boy and Warren. As the police officer climbed out of her car, Beth let go of my collar and raised her hands in the air. It was over.

The next day at school, the kids buzzed about the showdown at the cemetery. Some rumoured that the Gangstas rose from their graves to catch the Graffiti Ghouls. Others claimed I'd used kung fu to knock out bikers who were on a spray-painting spree. Trina put a stop to all the gossip and told the truth: Remi led Dough Boy and Warren on a wild goose chase through the trailer park so that she could get in his home and call the police. If it wasn't for Remi's fast feet and quick thinking, Trina would have never been able to call the cops, and I would have been mincemeat. Trina called him a hero, and Remi said that she was a heroine. The French girls apologised to Remi and followed him all over the school, while the Boissonault brothers punched him in the arm and told him he did a good job. The Rake apologised to Remi in front of everyone. He even took away Remi's strikes.

The Graffiti Ghouls didn't come from the trailer park like some kids suspected. They lived in the new suburbs of Bouvier, which put a stop to the rumours about criminals living in trailers, but this fact started brand new rumours about criminals who lived in the new suburbs. Gossip never went away; it just found new targets. I was glad that my friend's name had been cleared, but there was a price. Mom and Dad grounded me for a month because I hadn't gone home right after school like Mom said. But when they learned why, they cut my punishment to only two weeks.

As I headed home Remi and Trina caught up to me just outside the schoolyard.

"What's your rush?" he asked.

"Mom's got a ton of chores for me to do. Newton's Law is nothing compared to Mom's Justice," I said.

Remi chuckled.

"Maybe we can help," Trina said.

I shook my head. "I'm going to get lots of help. The Graffiti Ghouls have to clean off the paint and work at the store for a month."

Remi held his hand up for a high five. I smacked his palm in victory. Then I held my hand up, inviting Trina to give me a high five. She smiled shyly then whacked my hand so hard I thought she'd broken my bones.

"You're not so bad for a boy," Trina said.

"Ow." I rubbed my sore hand. "You mean I'm not so bad, period."

"Wimp," Remi teased. He held his hand up, and Trina smacked it hard. Crack! It sounded like car backfiring.

Remi flexed his hand, surprised.

"*Hel-lo.* Who's the wimp now?" Trina teased.

"I'm not a wimp," Remi said. "Snot gobbler."

He playfully hip-checked Trina, but she barely budged. Instead she hip-checked him, knocking him back three or four steps. He smiled admiringly at Trina, who laughed so sweetly it sounded like music. Sure she was bossy, nosy, and a shameless gossip, but she was also strong, smart, and fun when she wanted to be. She beamed at me, her lips no longer stained with slushies. The thought of kissing Trina didn't seem so bad now.

MARTY CHAN is a nationally known dramatist, screenwriter and author. He is the recent winner of the Edmonton Book Prize for this juvenile novel *The Mystery of the Frozen Brains* and former Gemini-nominated and gold-medal winner for *The Orange Seed Myth* and *Other Lies Mothers Tell.* His Canadian play *Mom, Dad, I'm Living With A White Girl* entertained audiences in Canada and abroad.